MYSTERY OF COYOTE CANYON

□□□ MYSTERY OF □□□
COYOTE
CANYON

Timothy Green

Illustrations by the Author

Ancient City Press
Santa Fe, New Mexico

International Standard Book Number
0-941270-83-1

Book Design by Mary Powell

Cover Illustration by Timothy Green
Cover Design by Connie Durand
Typography by Buffalo Publications

Green, Timothy.
Mystery of Coyote Canyon / Timothy Green.—1st ed.
    p.   cm.
Summary: While visiting the Navajo Reservation in Arizona, twelve-year-old Chris and new friend Anna learn many historical and prehistorical facts as they solve a mystery surrounding strange occurrences in Canyon de Chelly.
ISBN 0-941270-83-1
(1. Mystery and detective stories. 2. Navajo Indians—Fiction. 3. Indians of North America—Fiction.) I. Title.
PZ7.G82636Mu 1992
[Fic.]—dc20   93-44119
                                                         CIP
                                                          AC

10 9 8 7 6 5 4 3 2 1

For Dazhoni

*Special thanks to Ann Mason, David Seppa, and Shelley Voelkner
for their valued contributions to this story.*

Author's Note

All the characters in this story are a product of my imagination. Coyote Canyon is also ficticious, but Canyon de Chelly is very real. All the myths and stories of the Navajo are portrayed with as much authenticity as possible. The history is real. The ghosts? Well, wander through an ancient Indian ruin alone and after dark sometime . . .

—Timothy Green

CONTENTS

PART I: *Secrets of the Past*

PART II: *Secrets of the Present*

PART I

Secrets of the Past

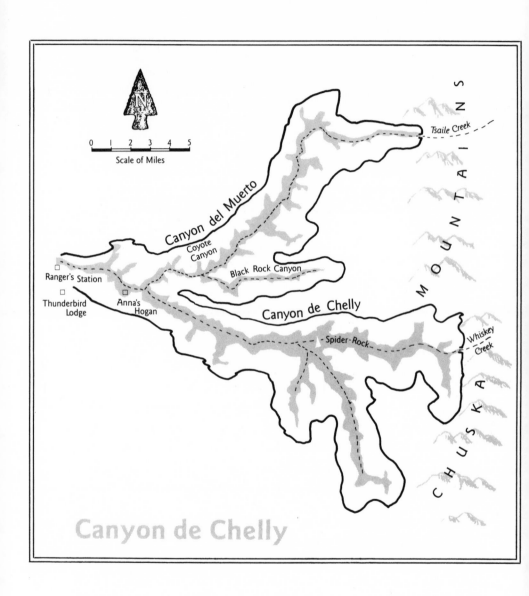

N

0 1 2 3 4 5
Scale of Miles

Canyon del Muerto

Coyote
Canyon

Black Rock Canyon

Ranger's Station

Thunderbird
Lodge

Anna's
Hogan

Canyon de Chelly

Spider-Rock

Tsaile Creek

Whiskey
Creek

M O U N T A I N S

C H U S K A

Canyon de Chelly

~~~~ **1** ~~~~

THE ROCKS HAVE EYES

S OMEONE'S UP THERE *watching us.*

Christopher Warren was certain. It was more than a hunch. It was a sixth sense, intuition you might call it. He could feel the eyes boring down on him. It made his skin crawl. Trying not to be too obvious, he scanned the cliff walls of the canyon: vastness. High above, an eagle soared in lazy circles, showing only a mild interest in the scene below.

It's your imagination. You're just being paranoid, he told himself. But he didn't believe a word of it.

The cliffs towered a thousand feet above as the three riders splashed through the sandy stream on the canyon floor. They rode in single file, each feeling reluctant to break the spell of the morning quiet. Chris noted that the sun had finally scaled the upper rim. Its rays painted thin washes of light along the edges of the streaked and hewn rock.

There! A darting movement. He was sure of it.

"Erick, hold up, will ya?"

The other two riders reined in their mounts and gazed back at him inquisitively. Both men wore the green and tan uniforms of National Park Rangers. They waited patiently until Chris's pinto nudged up against Erick's brown mare.

"I know this is going to sound crazy . . . but I think someone's up there spying on us."

Erick pulled off his hat and wiped an already sweating brow with his shirt sleeve. His blond, short-cropped hair glistened as he studied the ramparts above. Strong, calloused fingers held the reins of his mount lightly while the mare pranced in the streambed impatiently.

"Yeah. Right. I think your imagination's getting the best of you, buck-o," he said, grinning. "The Indians happen to have surrendered around here over a hundred years ago."

"The boy's right, Erick," said Kee. "The rocks have eyes. Someone's up there, though I haven't caught more than a glimpse of him yet. Whoever it is, he's pretty good at stalking."

Erick looked at his nephew, obviously impressed. He had too much respect for his Navajo friend to doubt the man's word on it. Kee Gorman had grown up here. His family had lived in the canyon for over two hundred years. His father had been one of the first Navajo rangers, and had taught Kee forestry as well as traditional *nahaghá*, the care of Mother Earth. If anyone knew this country, this canyon, it was Kee.

The Navajo's dark, penetrating eyes were appraising Chris. "Erick, the boy must be part Indian," he said. "Not too many men I know could do better at scouting."

Like most Navajo, Kee wasn't the type to hand out a compliment as free as candy. It had to be earned. Erick could see the pleased expression on his nephew's face. The boy's green eyes shone with pride.

Looking back, Erick had been a bit apprehensive about having his twelve-year-old nephew spend the summer with him at Canyon de Chelly. Erick considered himself a loner; he was unmarried, unattached to family life. He cherished his freedom. It was the

kind of freedom that allowed him to do his job wholeheartedly, without feeling tangled with other commitments. He loved his work, which often times amounted to twelve-maybe sixteen-hour days: patrolling the canyon, clearing trails that got buried beneath rock slides, mapping paths that lay hidden in the canyons, or just nurturing along young junipers that needed extra loving care. He was the confirmed bachelor, the real McCoy.

So it was not surprising that he had spent a whole evening several months back making a list of reasons why it would *not* be feasible to have his sister's son out for an extended visit. Janet had called him back in April, pleading with him to be open to the idea, for her sake, for Chris's sake, and so on. And on the phone he had cringed but said he'd consider it. He did—for about five seconds. Sure he felt bad for the kid, but he didn't need additional worries and couldn't afford to spend his summer wet-nursing anybody's boy, not even Janet's. He simply had too much work to do. Erick typed out a letter to Janet, giving numerous reasons why it wouldn't work, along with several suggestions of dude ranches they could look into. He signed off with ample apologies and stuffed the letter in an envelope—an unmailed envelope that was still in the bottom drawer of his desk.

For in the meantime, he had received a very direct and honest letter from Chris. The boy described the trouble at home, explained how he had saved up some money delivering newspapers, and how he was sure that his uncle would really rather not have him visit, but that his mom was hoping it would work out. He mentioned his parents' divorce, not as a plea for sympathy, but rather matter-of-factly, explaining that his mother was worried about how he was handling it. Chris went on to say that he would not be a bother but would be a willing partner in sharing Erick's work. Or if his uncle were concerned about having his own breathing space, Chris assured him that he enjoyed spending time alone, and it would not be necessary for Erick to be Chris's tour guide and entertainment center. Chris told how he loved to study about Indians, and that a summer vacation on the Navajo Reservation would be a perfect opportunity to do just that.

The straightforwardness of the letter impressed Erick. He hadn't seen Janet's son for almost five years, but he remembered that he had taken a liking to the boy back then. He had found Chris to be a quiet, rather serious kid. Not shy, Erick recalled. Instead, Chris had seemed deliberative, observing. His large, pensive eyes had followed Erick's every movement, his every gesture. So Erick reconsidered Chris's visit. Why not? Erick mused. It could turn out to be interesting. Besides, closer ties with Janet during this time were certainly called for. He had never thought much of his sister's choice of a husband, and the divorce confirmed his earlier suspicions. The guy had always seemed too hung up on himself, too selfish with *his* time, *his* work.

So the letter that was finally sent off to Minneapolis turned out to be an invitation. Erick wrote to Chris and Janet about what Chris could expect when he arrived: remoteness, primitive conditions. He explained that many of the roads on the reservation were not paved, were nothing more than tire-rutted trails that led from one settlement to another, and that these roads were often impassable after a summer thunderstorm. He described how most of the small homes that were scattered across the reservation still lacked plumbing, how water had to be hauled to homes from community wells. Telephones were scarce. In an area the size of Connecticut, the phone book for the entire reservation was less than half an inch thick. He mentioned that many Navajo still dwelled in hogans, small earth-covered huts without electricity, without modern comforts. Erick also sent along a map of Arizona, highlighting the route Chris would be taking through the northern part of the state, a route by bus from Flagstaff up to Chinle, the small community near Canyon de Chelly.

And now Erick was glad that it had all come about. A great relationship had already developed between them in the few days that Chris had been here. He glanced over at his nephew.

Chris was wearing a blue and white bandanna around his thick, brown hair. *Handsome kid*, Erick thought. He was aware that most people took an instant liking to his nephew. The boy's wide, sensitive mouth offered smiles easily, and others naturally responded.

It was Kee who brought Erick's attention back to matters at hand. "You know, if we want to lose our shadow up there, I figure all we'd have to do is shift into high gear and hit the gas. We'd have him eating our dust, pronto."

The idea apparently suited Erick. He turned to Chris, flashed a devilish grin, and shouted, "Jumpin' Jack Flash, it's a gas, gas . . . GAS."

With a flick of the reins, the horses bolted. Hooves kicked up sand in a spray of excitement as Chris's horse followed the two yelping riders. The canyon resounded with hoots, howls, and thundering horseflesh. Apprehension over the "spy" vanished.

A half mile down the wash, they brought their mounts to a check. The horses slowed to an easy gallop, then to a jarring trot, and finally to a walk. Chris could feel the heat rising off his animal. Ahead, stood a massive rock pointing hundreds of feet up from the sand. It looked like a giant tower guarding some crumbling world of the past.

Chris looked over his shoulder and studied the way they had come.

The canyon twisted in such a manner that less than a quarter mile of the wash was visible at any time. There was no sign of being followed. Although he tried not to think about it, he knew that the only way back to Thunderbird Lodge and the stables was the route they had ridden. The person lurking up in the rocks would be aware of that, too.

Kee and Erick seemed to have already forgotten the whole perplexing matter. They had dismounted and were rewarding their horses with lumps of sugar. Kee softly mentioned something to Erick, and they both smiled as Chris brought his own horse to a halt. Following their lead, he slipped out of the saddle and affectionately rubbed down his mount, searching his pocket for a sugar cube.

Kee pointed at the rock tower. Its uppermost tip was already touching sunlight. "The Navajo call this Spider Rock—it's connected with a legend as old as the *Diné*, the People," he said. "It's believed that Spider Woman, an ancient god, lives up there. She takes bad children to the top and leaves them. The white stones on the crown are said to be the sun-bleached bones of the unfortunate little ones. It goes without saying, not too many children wish to come here.

"Across the canyon is Talking Rock," Kee gestured. "It's a friend of Spider Rock's. Because Spider Woman can't see down the canyon to where the bad children are, she relies on Talking Rock to tell her."

Chris stood looking at the monstrous pinnacle with even greater appreciation. The story was make-believe, of course, but it was interesting. Like everything around here, he mused. Often reality was woven together with Navajo legends.

Sandwiches and canteens were uncovered from saddlebags, and they ate an early lunch since it would be a good three hours before they were back. Then they remounted the rested animals and began their trip home.

"Do you think we'll run into any trouble on our way home?" Chris asked as he tried not to sound too concerned.

"Trouble? There'll be no trouble," Kee promised. "This is sacred land to the *Diné* who live here. There's nothing to worry about."

Erick pointed to a pile of stone bricks heaped in a shallow grotto above the canyon floor. They looked like the remains of some old walls, now turned to mere rubble.

"Kee, tell our young friend here about these ruins."

The Navajo looked back at Erick, then turned around and rode on. Chris wondered if Kee had heard him or if he just didn't want to talk about it. They rode for a few minutes in silence; then unexpectedly, Kee began his account of the ruins.

"Within these walls dwelled a people of the past . . . long past. They were here before the *Diné*. There are those who say that they are still here. Their spirits linger among the stones."

Chris assumed Kee was teasing. But then again, something in the way the Indian spoke seemed to indicate otherwise. There was a faraway sound to his voice, like he was reciting a story that had been told and retold.

The Navajo ranger continued: "They are called the Anasazi—the Ancient Ones. Some say they were the Ancient Enemies. But this could not be. . . . They taught us how to grow corn and beans. Our grandparents of long ago sat at their fires and heard their stories. The Anasazi gave us gifts—strange birds from other lands, jewelry, and blankets. They built cities within the cliffs and throughout the canyons of this sacred land. Many are still standing, and they have become monuments of their past: Mesa Verde in Colorado, Chaco Canyon in New Mexico, Keet Seel and Betatakin in Arizona. Their beautiful pottery and their stone tools have been excavated through painstaking work by archaeologists and are now in museums as relics of their past glory. The Ancient Ones were skilled in their crafts and wise at surviving in this harsh land.

"But hundreds of years ago they mysteriously disappeared. Some say that drought drove them away, caused them to scatter into small bands that later became the Pueblo tribes of the Hopi, Zuni, and Acoma. Some say warring tribes from the north drove them away. And yet others say that the Anasazi crawled down into their kivas—their sacred chambers in the earth—and passed into another world."

Intrigued with this latest of strange tales, Chris rode in silence most of the way home. His imagination carried him back to the fascinating time that Kee had described. In his mind, he could smell the fires in the dwellings and hear the laughter and cries of the children, their echoes resounding against the stone walls. He wondered if anyone really believed that "the spirits still linger." *Maybe he means the memory of them still exists. No one believes in ghosts anymore, do they?*

Each rider drifted with his own thoughts, carried along by the rhythm of his horse's movements. It was Erick who again broke the silence.

"This is Canyon del Muerto that opens up on our right. It's the major tributary off the main canyon. We'll explore it on our next pack trip."

Chris turned. "It's so quiet—almost spooky."

"It's less traveled. It's also much narrower, which can make it seem a bit closed in and menacing. Kee could tell you some real hair-raisers about this place."

"More ghost stories?" Chris asked.

"Not ghost stories, war stories," Kee answered. "Canyon del Muerto is a Spanish name meaning 'Canyon of Death.' It's been called that ever since the massacre."

"Massacre?"

Erick explained: "In 1805, the Spanish military entered Canyon del Muerto to put a stop to Navajo raiding. There were about three hundred Spanish soldiers against a small band of Indians. The men, women, and children were crowded up high on a ledge when the soldiers attacked. When the first Spaniard climbed up to where they were, a young Indian woman threw herself at him to save her children. They both fell to their deaths. Most of the Navajo died there that day."

Shifting his weight in the saddle, Erick continued: "Due to their beliefs, the Navajo haven't touched anything up there that remains from the massacre. Other people, of course, have carted off everything from weapons to old bones as souvenirs."

"I've never known of a place with so many stories," Chris said thoughtfully.

"There's more, buck-o," Erick offered. "Kee, tell him about Coyote Canyon."

Again, the Navajo ranger seemed reluctant to volunteer information.

He slowly shook his head. "All right. I'll tell it as I've heard it.

"A little way up Canyon del Muerto are other tributaries that branch off," Kee explained. "One of these is a small, almost hidden gulch known as Coyote Canyon. It'd be considered unimportant in comparison to the larger ravines around here except for one thing—it's believed to be *haunted*. For as long as I can remember, people have been afraid to go in there. Unusual things happen—cattle, sheep, and horses disappear, strange sounds occur . . . the place is evil."

Kee's description of the haunted canyon provoked a meditative mood in all three riders. Being so absorbed with everything else Chris had almost forgotten the first event of the day. They were in sight of Thunderbird Lodge before he remembered to worry about their mysterious spy!

The sun was almost directly overhead. Noontime. After returning their tired horses to the care of the stable hands, Erick and Kee walked over to the Canyon de Chelly headquarters. Chris waved good-bye and headed back to his room at the lodge.

Rooms at the Thunderbird were originally for tourists only, but Erick and a couple of other rangers occupied rooms with small kitchenettes. Chris was renting a regular guest room, located right next to Erick's, furnished with a small bed, a TV, and a desk without a chair. The walls were pictureless, and the rugs on the floor were old and worn, but the place smelled fresh and was kept impeccably clean.

Throwing himself on his bed, Chris was too tired to even pull off his dusty Nikes. So much had happened in one morning that it seemed like he'd been out in the canyon for days. *All this talk about ancient Indians, massacres, and haunted canyons—let alone being spied on . . .*

He was soon sleeping and didn't awake until suppertime.

That evening Chris decided it would be a good time to get out his sketchbook and walk the short distance down to the mouth of the canyon. With only a few hours of daylight left, the shadows on the cliffs should be interesting, he thought. Erick had mentioned that he wouldn't be back until late, so Chris had plenty of time to kill. Collecting a handful of charcoal sticks and his worn, leatherbound sketchbook, he set off toward the entrance of Canyon de Chelly. He had always liked drawing. It was as if he could escape into the very thing he was sketching. And ever since fourth grade when his teacher, Mrs. Rosenquist, had read the story about Benjamin West, the famous American painter, he had wanted to be an artist. Besides, it seemed to run in the family. His mom painted. Large, abstract floral pictures were her specialty; yet Chris could hardly remember her selling any. Most were out in the garage, covered with old, dusty blankets.

Walking down the winding path, he again thought about the intriguing ride through the canyon. He'd have to write a letter to his best friend, Rick, and tell him all about it. Thinking about home brought other memories—some not so pleasant. *Divorce. The big D word. Don't think about it.* But he couldn't help it. He felt betrayed. He was angry with both of them. It seemed that every time they got together to discuss anything it ended in a big fight. It was like they hated each other. How could his own mom and dad say such mean things back and forth? And what a mess they'd made of everything.

What was his mother going to do now? Sure, Dad said he would still help with the bills and everything, but even so, Mom would have to get a job. And what could she do? She just seemed so helpless most of the time. Maybe he could think of a way to make some money so she wouldn't have to worry about it.

Without grandeur, the canyon's entrance opened up before him. The modest ridge was less than thirty feet high on either side, taking only minutes to climb. From there, the dark blue silhouette of the Chuska Mountains could be seen stretching across the horizon.

Further up, Chris discovered a small ledge protruding halfway between the upper ridge and the white streambed below. What looked like a trail descended to where the rock jutted out, providing a perfect panoramic view for his drawing. Cautiously, he began to work his way down the steep and rugged path.

The descent was slow and difficult. His shadow, stretching out like a giant gargoyle, splattered on the boulders in front of him. Without warning, he heard a shower of loose gravel falling down from somewhere above. Small stones bounced and plummeted overhead. Surprised, he shielded his head with his sketchbook until the small avalanche was over.

Someone's up there. The feeling Chris had had earlier in the day returned. Again he was being watched, being followed. But this time he was alone. Craning his neck, he searched the rim above. *The rocks have eyes.* Sunlight glared back at him, making him squint.

A movement caught his eye and then disappeared. Something in the black shadow behind an outcrop had moved slightly. Suppressing panic, he began working his way back up the ravine, choosing a route which angled away from whoever was up there. Scrambling upward as best as he could, he made slow progress. Steep sandstone walls thwarted any attempt at speed. Panting, he heard someone getting closer.

Suddenly, he slipped on loose rock and began to slide backwards, scraping his hands and knees on the grainy sandstone surface. After a few heartpounding seconds, he slid to a stop.

Chris picked himself up; his knees were shaking. Puffing even harder, he brushed off his jeans and tried to calm himself. Again he heard loose stones falling. Whoever it was, they would soon meet. *Too late to get away.* He took a deep breath and picked up a rock, deciding to meet his adversary face-to-face.

An endless minute later, Chris heard the crunch of gravel underfoot. He was suddenly standing in shadow. Peering up into the sun, he could barely make out the dark figure looming above him.

~~~~ *2* ~~~~

ANNA JOE

CHRIS WAS BOTH SURPRISED and relieved to find that it was only a Navajo girl. He guessed her to be about his age, small boned and tiny, but imposing from where she stood.

After an interim of scrutinizing each other, he realized that it would have to be his initiative to break the silence.

"Hi," he stammered, his voice sounding tiny.

No response.

"I hope I'm not trespassing—I came up here to do some drawing . . . "

The girl just stood there holding a rifle, which certainly didn't help break the ice.

" . . . and I'm fine. Thanks for your concern."

Still no response. She just stared at him, her long, black hair blowing like wisps of smoke in the wind. She was both tomboyish and pretty, with dark, almond-shaped eyes and a mouth that seemed to pout.

"Do you live around here?" he asked, instantly realizing what a silly question that was. He was feeling more awkward by the minute.

"Well, it's been great talking to you," he said wryly. "Maybe I'll see you around."

But even as he turned to go, he knew their encounter wasn't over.

"You *are* trespassing," the girl announced.

"I'm sorry. I didn't . . . I mean, I wish . . . "

"If wishes were fishes, we'd all cast nets."

What a strange girl, Chris thought. Certainly not the sweet, timid type.

"You were trespassing this morning, too. You're a *bilagáana*. You have no right riding in this canyon—it doesn't belong to you!"

He gaped at her: "So you're the spy!"

She smiled for the first time. "Of course. I'm in charge of watching over everything around here. I'm sort of like the guardian of this place."

Chris suspected she was lying. But lying or not, he was relieved to discover that her rifle was only a BB gun. He studied her closely, noticing the patches on her jeans. Her clothes were worn and faded, but clean.

He attempted one last time to smooth things over. He still had to squint into the sun to see her.

"I didn't mean any harm. My name is Christopher Warren. My friends call me Chris. I'm from Minneapolis. That's in . . . "

"I know where it is," she interrupted. "It's along the Mississippi River in Minnesota, with another city . . . St. Paul. St. Paul is the capital."

Again, Chris found himself at a loss. She obviously didn't suffer from lack of education.

"Who are you?" he asked, frowning.

"I'm a Navajo *princess*," she answered. "My grandfather is a powerful medicine man; he's teaching me his strong medicine. I will use my powers to protect my grandmother's sheep from the spirits in the canyon."

The mention of spirits pricked Chris's interest.

"You mean the spirits in the *haunted* canyon?"

It was now her turn to look puzzled. "Who told you about the haunted canyon?"

"A ranger friend of mine—a Navajo. Kee Gorman."

Anna lowered her eyes for a moment, then glanced at the over-sized watch on her small wrist and said, "I've got to go now."

Before Chris could think of anything else to say, the girl slipped around a large rock and disappeared. Suddenly, he was alone again, in total silence, and feeling quite puzzled. If he didn't know better, it could've all been an apparition, he thought, as he started back toward the lodge.

And a strange apparition at that.

It was dark by the time he made it back to the Thunderbird. The moon, an oversized silver disk, bobbed along the skyline, looking plump enough to drop. Chris couldn't take his eyes off it. Even though he hadn't been able to draw, the evening had been most interesting. He noticed Erick's Jeep wasn't parked out front yet, which meant his uncle was still out.

On the way to his room he saw a big Navajo woman leaving the kitchen and walking toward the parking lot. Chris recognized her immediately: "Marie!" he hailed.

Marie turned and waved as Chris jogged over to her.

"How's my young man tonight?" she greeted. "And out so late. Don't you know that *adiltgá shii* come out at night? You're walking around here like live bait!"

"Adil—what?"

"*Adiltgá shii.* Skinwalkers. Navajo witches. Many of my people believe that they roam around here at night. They're skin changers. They can become a wolf, or an owl. But we shouldn't talk of such things out here in the dark. . . . So what keeps a young boy out this late at night?"

Chris would have to find out more about skinwalkers later. Right now, there was something else he needed to know.

"Marie, what is a bellagun?"

She gave him an odd look. "A what?"

"A bellagun, or something like that. Someone said I was a bellagun."

"A *bilagáana*," she laughed. "That means a white person."

"Oh," Chris muttered, half to himself. That wasn't so bad. "Marie, do you know anything about a Navajo princess living around here?"

Another odd look from Marie.

"I met a girl tonight who said she was a princess," he explained, feeling a bit foolish now as he thought about it.

"A Navajo princess, huh?" she smiled. "There ain't no royal blood around here but mine. That's right! Didn't you know? I'm the Queen of Sheba."

This tickled her, and she laughed heartily at her own joke.

Chris liked Marie. He liked her cheerful, motherly way. She could be terribly domineering in the kitchen, yet her love for laughing betrayed a warm heart. But right now Chris was feeling pretty silly for being so gullible.

Marie, sensing his embarrassment, wrapped a heavy arm around his shoulders. "There's no such thing as Navajo princesses, child. Don't believe everything you hear around here. Some people have nothing better to do than spin yarns. This princess of yours is nothing more than a screwball kid with a couple of nuts loose. I've seen my share."

The next morning, Chris was up early enough to have breakfast with his uncle in the lodge's cafeteria, where Mr. Murray, the manager of the Thunderbird, joined them. Chris guessed Mr. Murray to be in his fifties. He was a big man, with a high, sunburned forehead and close-cropped, graying hair. He had a large handlebar mustache that collected small particles of toast as he ate.

"This is a country filled with legends and superstitions," he lectured philosophically. "Spirits are so much a part of everyday living around here that I'm sure a lot of Navajo don't make any distinction between reality as we know it and the supernatural.

"Their whole culture is rich in tales of magic," he continued, belaboring his point. "Everything we Anglos declare to be natural phenomena—the wind, thunder, the sun, the rain—these are the divine beings, the Holy People to the Navajo. I tell you, Navajo reality takes on a whole different meaning."

Erick looked up from his plate and grinned. "Speaking of different perspectives on reality, what's this I hear about a Navajo princess?"

Chris felt like sliding under the table. So Marie had told Erick about his encounter with the strange girl.

"I guess I was really taken for a ride," he mumbled. He forked a large piece of egg and lifted it part way to his mouth. "It seemed believable enough at the time; she seemed so confident and proud, like . . . "

Mr. Murray winked. "Well, maybe in the youngster's eyes she was a princess."

Chris was getting more embarrassed by the second. He knew it would be too much to expect the grown-ups to just drop it; he'd better find a way to change the subject.

"I saw Kee this morning," he said. "He mentioned something about inviting me out to his aunt and uncle's home for dinner."

"That's right," Erick confirmed. "You and I are to be his guests tonight. Kee's aunt and uncle live right in the canyon . . . very primitive. It should be quite an experience for you."

Erick pushed out his chair and stood up, grabbing his plate and polishing off a glass of milk simultaneously. "Look, I've got to run— I'll pick you up around 6:00. See you guys later. Oh yeah, Chris, let me know if you run into any more princesses, huh? Maybe you could line me up with one around my age."

Mr. Murray laughed and also stood up to leave. He patted Chris on the shoulder, grumbled something about always having work to do, and headed off toward the kitchen.

So now Chris had the day to himself. Thinking of his plans that were thwarted yesterday, he decided to venture once again to the mouth of the canyon to draw. He would be careful not to wander in too far though; he remembered that Erick had told him just about the same thing that the girl had mentioned yesterday: white people were not allowed into Canyon de Chelly without being accompanied by a Navajo. That was because the canyon was sacred to them.

The day passed quickly. His time on the rim was productive artistically but otherwise uneventful. There wasn't any sign of the Navajo princess, nor was there any evidence of disappearing cattle or restless spirits. By the time Erick picked him up that evening, Chris doubted if things were much different around Canyon de Chelly than they

were at home. All the talk about spirits and magic was probably
nothing but a bunch of superstitious nonsense, he thought.

"You're awfully quiet," Erick observed, casting a quick glance at his
nephew as they drove along the floor of the canyon. The road in the
canyon demanded full attention since there was always a good chance
of getting bogged down in quicksand. Chris only smiled. A little ways
up from a wash, a spattering of peach trees and cottonwoods dotted
the area. Three miles into the chasm, they turned right and headed
up Wild Cherry Canyon. Almost immediately after their turn, Erick
maneuvered the Jeep into a rutted driveway and slowed to a near stop.
Evidently they had arrived.

Chris recognized Kee's pickup parked next to another, older truck.
Both vehicles were a short distance away from the hogan, the traditional Navajo home.

The hogan was made of logs laid horizontally, forming a hexagon.
Logs which were chinked with adobe mud also covered the dome-
like roof. Chris noticed that the door faced east, as was customary.
Kee had mentioned to him earlier that the Navajo believed that all
gifts and blessings came with the rising of the sun, so the door of a
traditional hogan always faced in that direction. The Navajo ranger
had thoroughly explained the significance of the hogan to Chris: "We
believe that at the time of creation, the gods first created the hogan,
and then the order and planning of other things followed. Hogans
are sacred. Even the materials used for building them are carefully
chosen. Only logs untouched by lightning can be used, because those
that have been struck are already the property of lightning. A hogan
must also be built in a carefully chosen spot—not too close to anthills
or places where lightning has struck. After it is built, the beams are
annointed with cornmeal during a Blessing Way ceremony. A
medicine man is hired to do that; he must touch each post with
cornmeal, walking through the hogan clockwise, in the direction
of the sun's rising and setting, the sacred direction of order within
the cosmos."

They came to a complete stop about thirty yards from the other
trucks. Erick turned off the ignition and sat with his hands folded

and resting on the steering wheel.

"You should never park in front of a hogan door," he explained. "It's considered bad manners. Usually, a hogan is built as only one room. If the door's open, you'd be able to see if anyone is home. If there's someone there and they don't want company, they simply won't come out. So it's better you don't know if anyone's there or not; that way, everyone saves face.

"Another thing," Erick continued, "don't get out of your vehicle right away—wait awhile. Someone will come out if they want to see you; if not, they won't."

Sure enough, in a moment the door opened and out stepped Kee. An elderly couple appeared behind him and stood watching as Kee approached the two guests.

"Ya et éh," Kee greeted, shaking their hands. "Please come and introduce yourselves to my aunt and uncle. The old man's name is Davidson—Davidson Charley; his wife's is Arletta."

Davidson Charley was a small, weathered-looking man who wore his long, gray hair tied back in a bun. He was crowned in a tall, black Stetson, which was accented with a beautifully beaded headband. His clothes were old and faded, contrasting with the shiny silver necklace around his neck. He held out a gnarled hand that Chris accepted.

"Ya et éh," Chris stammered, hoping that his pronunciation wasn't too awful to understand.

Mr. Charley shook his hand lightly, smiling, without acknowledging if he understood Chris's greeting or not.

"Ya et éh," declared the musical voice of the short, plump woman standing beside him. Chris looked down into her beaming face and couldn't help but feel welcomed. Arletta spoke again in her melodious Navajo and laughed.

The old woman was clothed in the traditional long satin skirt with a mauve-colored velvet blouse, a sight not uncommon here, especially among the older people. Her wrists were adorned with heavy turquoise and silver bracelets. She also wore her hair tied back, wrapped in a neat bun with heavy wool string.

After formal introductions were out of the way, Chris and his uncle were escorted into the hogan. The first thing Chris noticed was that the only light coming into the room was from the smoke hole in the center of the roof, where a stovepipe extended to the outside. After he allowed his eyes to adjust to the darkness for a second, he observed Erick moving around the dwelling from left to right, clockwise—the sacred direction of order—circling the iron stove in the middle and sitting down on the west side, facing the entrance. Realizing it must be customary, Chris followed in like manner.

While the others entered, he looked around the humble little hogan. He could now make out most of the details in the room. To the right of the entrance, simple shelves made of orange crates were stacked with dishware and food staples. On the other side, sheepskins were rolled and stacked neatly on the earthen floor. There was no furniture except for the worn old couch on which he sat and a couple of vinyl-covered dining chairs that looked forlornly out of place.

With Kee interpreting from time to time, conversation ran surprisingly smooth. They talked about the weather: the lack of rain for this time of season, the wells that were drying up on parts of the reservation. After awhile, discussion turned to the old man.

In broken English, Davidson Charley talked about himself: "My whole life I have walked the medicine path. When I was a boy, I learned the simple healing ceremonies. When I grew older, I learned the harder ones. Some things took me years to learn. I know of cures that few others know.

"The old stories of my ancestors were passed on to me by my father," the old man continued. "There is power in these stories. I learned about the *Diyin Dinée*, the Holy Beings. I was taught the Beauty Way stories of White Shell Woman and her twins: Monster Slayer and Born-for-the-Water. I learned the ways of walking in harmony with Mother Earth and Father Sky."

Arletta opened the old cast-iron stove and carefully removed a covered pan. With pot holder mittens she peeled away the upper wrapping, exposing the meal for the evening.

"Navajo tacos," she said with a smile.

Large helpings were heaped onto plastic plates and handed around the room. Coffee, milk, and sodas were offered. Chris accepted a warm Coke—there wasn't a refrigerator in the Charley home. After Kee blessed the food in Navajo, they began their dinner.

It was delicious, Chris thought. The Navajo taco was made up of bits of lamb with a thick sauce of refried beans. He couldn't recognize the spices except for the green chile. The whole concoction was folded into a large, round piece of bread fried in bacon grease, called Indian fry bread.

Before long, Chris was sitting back against the wall feeling very full. He offered to help with dishes but was glad to be refused. Arletta explained that since it was such a big job, she only washed her dishes once a day. Washing them consisted of filling a large basin with water from the well and then heating it over an open fire. The process could wait till morning.

Chris peered out past the door which stood slighty ajar. Transluscent light grew opaque. Inside, Kee switched on the single light near the doorway, causing shadows to leap away from its unnatural glow. Chris was thinking that it must be about time to go when he heard someone approaching.

The door swung open with a bang, and a rush of energy blew in. A girl followed.

"You must excuse our granddaughter for being so late," Arletta apologized. "She's always in a hurry but never seems to be on time. Child, how could it take you all evening to round up a few sheep?"

The girl held her head down; long lashes concealed her eyes. It was obvious from the blush in her cheeks that she was feeling uncomfortable being the focus of attention. She really didn't look too remorseful, Chris thought. Actually, she looked like she was trying to cover a smile. When she looked up, her dark eyes danced.

Standing in front of him, smiling coyly, was the girl he had met in the canyon.

Her hair was now braided into two long pigtails which almost touched her waist. She, too, was clothed in traditional wear: moccasins and a brown velvet blouse with matching satin skirt. It was the dress reserved for ceremonies, Chris observed, or special occasions such as entertaining guests.

Arletta smiled and shook her head. "This is Anna Joe, our grand-daughter. She lives with us now. You're not always this shy, are you, Anna?"

Anna stood with her head bowed, fumbling with a loose thread on her blouse. Chris found it difficult to believe that this seemingly shy, quiet girl was the same bold defender of the canyon. *The Navajo princess.*

Remembering how she had caused him embarrassment only this morning, he couldn't help but retaliate.

"This is the girl who told me that she was a Navajo princess," Chris offered innocently enough, yet hoping for the right response. He smiled mirthlessly.

Again, all eyes were on Anna. *The right response.* Chris could almost feel her squirming. He was actually a bit sorry he'd been so anxious to get even.

"But I guess I had it coming," he countered, "being hoodwinked. I was quite the klutz up on the rocks, and I might've fallen off if someone hadn't chased me out of there."

Anna looked up from the floor, and their eyes met for a second.

Kee said something to the girl in Navajo, and she shrugged.

Davidson Charley laughed. The wrinkles around his eyes curved into upward lines. "She's a very different child, my Anna. She carries too much on her small shoulders. I've asked her to keep watch of the sheep and to report back to me.

She takes her responsibilities too seriously. Instead of playing with other children, she works and she protects."

All this attention fixed on the girl who claimed to be a princess was too much for her. Quietly, she asked permission to gather firewood and retreated toward the door.

"Would you mind if I come with you?" Chris asked.

Anna appeared pleased that he'd asked, so he followed her. As they walked toward the woodpile, Chris could still hear the drone of conversation coming from inside the hogan. He was glad to be out in the fresh air. The moon was shining in full, casting a pale glow on a flock of sheep close by.

"I'm sorry for embarrassing you in there," he said, actually meaning it.

Anna laughed aloud under a juniper tree. A grazing sheep looked at her balefully.

"I guess I had it coming. I was very mean to you yesterday."

"That's okay," he said, wanting to forget about it.

"Your grandparents are awfully nice."

She smiled. "I know. They're good to me."

"Yesterday I mentioned that I knew Kee—why didn't you tell me he was your uncle?"

"You never asked," she said, teasing.

They stood there for a time in silence, peering up at the stars which were beginning to pop out. To Chris's surprise, Anna began humming a tune, soft and melodious. When she had finished, the night seemed especially quiet.

"That was cool."

Anna shrugged. "We Navajo have many songs. There are sacred songs, songs for ceremonies and for celebrating. A medicine man like my grandfather must know all of them. There are songs about all living creatures: songs of protection, to ward off evil, songs about the Four Sacred Mountains and about this canyon. There are sad songs and songs for fun.

A Navajo feels rich according to how many songs he knows. Thanks to my grandfather, I'm a very rich person."

Chris found himself liking this girl. He had been right—she was different, but different in a good way. She could be poetic, or she could be tough as nails.

"How come you live with your grandparents?" he asked.

Anna's face suddenly clouded over.

Chris could have kicked himself. They were just beginning to be friends, and he might have already blown it. Why did he have to ask so many dumb questions?

"I'm really sorry—again. I shouldn't be so nosey."

"That's okay. It's no secret. Both my parents died about a year ago . . . a car accident. A drunk driver ran into them."

"Jeez, I'm so sorry."

Anna looked at him. He truly looked sorry. She smiled.

"Did my uncle Kee really tell you about the haunted canyon?" she asked, changing the subject.

Chris nodded. "It's hard to know what to believe around here, but he did say some place nearby is supposed to be haunted."

"You don't believe it?"

He shrugged.

"It's true," she confirmed. "Everybody around here knows about it. Someday I'm going to go into Coyote Canyon—I'll show that I'm not afraid. No one's willing to go in there with me except Bill."

"Who's Bill?"

My best friend. He knows Canyon de Chelly better than anybody."

"Well," Chris ventured, "if you ever need a third party, I'd be willing to check the place out with you."

She stared at him for a moment. "Would you?"

Hearing voices outside the hogan, Chris could now see Erick in the doorway, shaking hands and getting ready to leave. On cue, he picked up a bundle of chopped wood and started back. Anna followed, carrying only a few small kindling chips.

After the farewells and thank-yous were said, Chris and Erick headed back to Thunderbird Lodge. That night, Chris dreamed. *Dreamed of a hogan in a deep canyon. A hogan with a stovepipe protruding from a small hole in the roof. Black smoke belched from the stovepipe and drifted up into the sky. Black smoke smothered the red moon and wrapped itself around the trees below, like long, withered fingers, choking . . . strangling . . . An old, gnarled juniper writhed under the sooty vapors and ash . . . An old juniper, on which hung a rotting sign . . . It was hard to read the sign . . . looked like a skull painted on it . . . a skull that leered at him as the sign swayed back and forth . . . back and forth . . . It swung from a branch that swayed in the suffocating moonlight . . . knocked back and forth against the trunk . . . knocked . . . it was hitting his window . . . knocking . . . faster and harder . . .*

Chris woke befuddled by the knocking—it was against his window. Someone was rapping against it in earnest. Fear touched his heart for a second; confused and disoriented, he slid his pajamaed legs over the side of the bed and scurried to the glass.

Outside it was black and still. Chris stood there, stunned, looking past his own reflection. For the third time in less than two days, he was staring at the girl named Anna Joe.

~~~ 3 ~~~

COYOTE CANYON

"TAKE A PICTURE, it'll last longer," Anna whispered through the window screen. "Hurry and get dressed. I'll be waiting over in the parking lot. Oh yeah, bring a jacket."

Without further explanation, Anna disappeared. Chris felt dazed. Switching on the light, he stood squinting and rubbing his eyes. *My clothes—where are my clothes? Okay. Jacket . . . okay. Is there a sane explanation for all this?*

By the time he slipped out the door and headed in the direction of the parking lot, he was feeling more awake. *What in the heck's going on?* A thin patch of moonlight disappeared under dark, ominous clouds. *It must be the middle of the night . . . DARN! Forgot my watch . . .*

Turning the corner, Chris was facing the gift shop's parking lot. Naturally, it was dark and empty, except for a few vacant pickup trucks. A single lamppost glimmered eerily at the far corner. Under the illumination was Anna. Amused, he saw that she was straddling an old, beat-up-looking motorcycle.

She was dressed in jeans and a jean jacket; her hair fell loosely over her shoulders. Under her arm she held a cycle helmet; attached to the back of the cycle was another. Looking at her, Chris saw little that resembled the girl he had been visiting only hours ago.

"I didn't think you were old enough to be driving one of these," he greeted.

The quick, darting eyes were certainly familiar.

"I'm not. This used to be my father's. Grandfather lets me drive it as long as I promise to stay off the roads."

"I suppose he never thought of a *time* restriction."

The sarcasm escaped her. He couldn't help but smile.

"What's so funny?"

"Nothing. So what's up? This an invite for a joy ride?"

"Hardly. You mentioned you were interested in Coyote Canyon . . . we're going there."

Chris shot her a surprised look.

"My aunt lives in Black Rock Canyon," Anna explained. "It's just across the wash from Coyote Canyon. Last night, after you left, she came over to see my grandfather. She was really scared. She told us that she had been rounding up sheep out there. It was already getting dark, when it all started—loud thundering sounds. Next, she said she saw fires falling from the sky and lighting up all over. There were evil spirits—*chindi*, flying all over the place.

Catching her breath, Anna continued: "My grandparents were finally able to calm her down, but it was already real late. She's now spending the night with us. When I was sure everyone was asleep, I got dressed and sneaked out. I walked my motorcycle far enough away so they wouldn't hear me start—it's an old trick of mine—and here I am."

A big, brown dog appeared out of nowhere and ambled over to where Chris was standing. He sniffed at Chris's shoes and then sat down near the front tire of the cycle.

"This is my friend, Bill," Anna introduced.

Is she kidding? Chris was learning better than to think so.

The dog looked up at him as if he knew he was being introduced. He actually appeared to be smiling, his eyes hinting that he expected a reward.

"Does his tongue always hang out like that?"

"Only when he's trying to make a good impression," she quipped.

Anna jumped up and kick-started the old motorcycle. A loud whine, turning to a low rumble, filled the parking lot.

"How did you know where to find me?" Chris asked, trying to recall if he had mentioned his room number to her earlier.

"Kee said something about it last night. What did you think, that I had you followed?" Anna grinned. "Here, put this on and hop on back," she said, slipping on her own helmet. The helmets were the modern kind, looking like they ought to be worn by astronauts rather than cyclists. Chris had barely climbed aboard when the cycle took off with a jump. Gripping the seat tightly, he was careful to keep his leg a healthy distance away from the hot muffler.

The motorcycle sputtered and whined as they bounced down the trail toward the canyon entrance. A single high beam of light danced in front of them, making rocks and trees appear like a slow-motion movie. Hitting a bump, the engine backfired loudly.

By the time they were in the canyon, Chris was glad he'd brought his jacket. It was surprisingly cold. Mist blanketed the wash, making visibility close to zero. Anna must be navigating on pure instinct, he thought.

Yes, Mrs. Warren. This is the Navajo Police. Did you know where your son was last night? No . . . no-sir-ee, not safe in his bed at the lodge, not last night! That's right . . . your son. Yeah, we had an accident here . . . messy. Looks like he was the passenger on a motorcycle driven by some crazy Navajo princess. We had to peel the kids off the trail . . . Yeah, that's right . . . nasty business . . .

Racing onward, the engine was backfiring nonstop, threatening to quit but never keeping its promise. Chris's hands were frozen. The motorcycle gyrated madly when it ran into deep sand, forcing passenger and driver to shift their balance like dancers.

After an eternity, the cycle wound down to a stop. Anna switched off the engine. Chris noticed two things as he pulled off his helmet and hobbled away from the cycle: It was dead quiet, and it was also about to rain. He felt a drop touch his cheek. Anna pulled the cycle back on its stand and turned off the headlight, leaving them in darkness. Real darkness. Darkness that can only be experienced when standing at the bottom of a canyon on a cloudy night, trying to decide if the place was really haunted or not.

Chris was transfixed. A sinister shape half hidden by juniper at the foot of an outcrop became, as his eyes adjusted better to the darkness, an oddly eroded boulder. He stared at the ghostly silhouettes all around. Giant pinnacles and weird rock formations were everywhere, making the place look like it had been imported from some other planet.

"Well, what now?" he said, trying to sound impatient.

Suddenly lights, or small fires, started to blink on and off at the far end of the mist-filled canyon. A pounding noise, at first sounding distant, then growing louder and nearer, increased to a booming thunder, reverberating against the cliff walls. It was like nothing Chris had ever heard. Something tightened around his chest. He looked at Anna. The effect on her had been electric. She stood staring into the canyon, her eyes wide with fear.

"R-r-restless spirits!" she cried.

Feeling both frightened and curious, Chris sought a logical explanation for all this. *What was going on in here? A helicopter? UFOs? A hoax?*

The lights gathered into a large mass, grew brighter, and then rose into the air. They disappeared. The pounding rhythm grew fainter and fainter.

Chris and Anna stood speechless. Even Bill looked perturbed by the whole situation.

"Incredible! Do you think it was a UFO?" Chris asked.

"A what?"

"You know, a flying saucer or something."

Anna shook her head. "It's *chindi*—ghosts from the dead."

A cock crowed somewhere in the early darkness. Lightning lit the upper rim of the canyon; its thunder rumbled a promise of rain.

Anna peered upward. "We'd better start back—it doesn't look good. The last thing we need right now is to be stuck here during a flash flood. Bill . . . let's go! Bill!"

Once again they bounced and skidded through the sandy gulch. Chris was feeling a little more adept at being a cycle passenger; he shifted his weight this way and that as they made their way back to the lodge.

By the time he reached his room, he was more than a little tired—he was exhausted. In bed, with security wrapped around him like a second blanket, he told himself there had to be a logical explanation for everything that had happened tonight. *There's no such thing as ghosts.* As he drifted off to sleep, it began to rain.

The next day, Anna pulled up to the curb while Chris was still trying to explain to himself what exactly he had seen in Coyote Canyon. Today they would try to find out. He waved and ran over to meet her, equipped with his sketchbook and pencils. He didn't have a camera, but at least he could record anything they saw with pencil and paper. Hopping on the back of the cycle, the tightness in his chest returned.

"Onward, my dear Watson!"

She turned. "What?"

"Forget it."

He noticed that Bill was close by, looking very much in need of a bath since the morning's rain. The dog greeted him with a friendly wag of his scraggy tail. *What a ragamuffin,* Chris chuckled to himself.

The cycle revved to a high pitch, then bucked like a bronco leaving its chute. The ground slipped away under their feet, and they were soon riding through Canyon de Chelly. Since it was impossible to talk over the noise of the engine, both riders concentrated on maneuvering around obstacles until they were once again in the strange and possibly haunted ravine.

Anna lifted the cycle to its stand, and they tied their helmets to the handlebars. Chris noticed that they were standing in nearly the same place they had been last night. It didn't seem as frightening during the day, but it still had an eeriness about it that was unnerving.

Peering into the chasm, he could see it was a box canyon. There was only one way in or out, unless there were ancient Indian trails hidden amongst the rocks, like the ones Erick had mentioned. He had said that in some places there were passageways that ascended seemingly sheer cliffs. The Anasazi had used small toe- and hand-holds carved into the rock for getting around.

It's actually quite pretty in here, Chris thought. Yucca and squash bush dotted the canyon floor. Junipers and piñons grew in sparse patches along a dried-up streambed. He even noticed a few desert flowers popping out here and there, saturated with sun in the brilliant light. Surprisingly, the sheer cliff at the end of the arroyo wasn't more than a half mile from where they stood. He had expected the canyon to be much deeper.

They began snooping around, searching for anything that might help explain what they had experienced last night. Bill nosed around, too, looking like he wasn't really sure what he was investigating but happy to be helping out. It was Anna who made the first find.

"Chris, look at this!" she exclaimed, holding up a broken shard of pottery.

Chris walked over to examine it. The piece wasn't any larger than a half-dollar. It was triangular in shape, grayish white, with a simple geometric pattern painted on it.

"Do you think this has anything to do with what happened last night?" he asked.

"Who knows? It might. Look, here's more—lots more."

Sure enough, the ground was littered with broken bits of pottery. Most of it was sticking out of the sandy streambed. It was fun picking up the shards and examining the various designs. Most were bold black-on-white patterns, filled with a closely spaced hatching.

"Is this Navajo pottery?"

"No way. This is Anasazi stuff. It's real old. My grandfather says that they lived around here over eight hundred years ago."

"How can you be so sure it's Anasazi?" Chris asked, somewhat skeptically.

"It's all over Canyon de Chelly. Old Navajo pottery's not this pretty; it's almost always earth-colored and plain; it never has these sorts of handpainted designs on it. The museum at the Ranger's Station has some Anasazi pots for the tourists to look at; go and check them out sometime."

Anna noticed Chris slipping a piece into his pocket.

"I wouldn't do that if I were you," she warned. "There are laws against taking any of this—you could be fined thousands of dollars. Besides that, archaeologists are always around here studying it. They say it's real important that none of this stuff is disturbed or stolen. It would be like taking away a little piece of a puzzle that could never be replaced.

"Most Navajo won't mess with it," she continued. "They're superstitious. They think that if they handle it, evil spirits, the *chindi* that hang around the dead, will hurt them—make them sick or cause bad things to happen to them."

"What about you—do you believe that?" he asked, as he dropped the small collection of shards he had picked up.

She shrugged. "I don't know . . . sometimes. Sometimes not. When I'm with my grandparents or at ceremonies, it's easy to believe in that way. When I'm in this canyon, surrounded by all the stories of Spider Woman and the Holy People, it's really easy to believe. But when I'm at school with other kids, it's easy to kind of laugh at the old beliefs."

They continued hiking up the canyon.

"You see this flat rock?" Anna pointed out. "It's an old milling stone. We call it by its Spanish name: a *metate*. The Anasazi pecked out the top like this to make a sort of basin out of it. They would grind seeds like corn and beans in here, crushing them with a small rock, the *mano*."

Following the dried-up wash as it curved toward the left side of the chasm, they approached the end of the canyon. It opened up much wider than it appeared from the entrance, and unexpectedly, a cluster of ruins loomed overhead, clutching the cliff about thirty feet above their heads. With towers commanding its periphery, the buildings clung to the huge crevice. The remains of what was apparently a wall twisted around the outer fringe of the structures.

"Looks like we hit the jackpot!" Chris shouted.

It didn't take long to notice that Anna wasn't as excited.

"What's the matter? Isn't this great!"

"You're forgetting what we're supposed to be doing here. This proves that I'm right—there *are* restless spirits haunting this place."

"Just because these old ruins are here doesn't mean there are evil spirits hanging around. I don't believe in such things."

Anna shook her head. "I'll bet they're real, and I'll bet they're here all right. I must be crazy for coming into Coyote Canyon in the first place."

The cliff dwellings were accessible only by ladders or by toe- and handholds which were difficult and dangerous to climb. Chris made a halfhearted if not foolhardy attempt for awhile but gave up. Anna seemed relieved.

"Let's look around some more and see if we can find where those fires were," Chris said. "We should at least be able to find some scorched areas."

"Not if they were spirits."

He ignored her remark and made his way over to another area. What a great place to show Erick, he thought. All this craziness about haunted canyons was probably nonsense. There had to be a logical explanation. The thundering sounds they had heard last night could've been thunder, echoing and sounding louder. The lights were probably small fires set off by lightning. The mist could've bounced the lights from the fires up into the sky. That would all make sense.

A cry from Anna brought his attention back to the present. He jogged over to where she knelt in the sand.

"I found one!" she beamed.

"Found what?"

"Look."

Anna held up a small piece of agate.

Chris picked it up and felt the carefully chipped edges. There was no mistaking that the stone was a finely crafted arrowhead.

"That's really cool!"

"It's beautiful. It's only the second one I've ever found."

"Well, if you're afraid of catching some evil spirits from it, I'll take it off your hands," Chris said with a grin.

"No way," she replied.

"But what about the antiquity laws and all that? Doesn't that apply to arrowheads, too?"

Anna shrugged. "My grandfather says if you find an arrowhead and it's not pointing at you, it's okay to pick it up." She began to inspect the ground even closer. Chris smiled to himself at her inconsistencies and shook his head.

They searched further in hopes of finding another arrowhead but soon concluded that Anna must have discovered the only one left in the whole canyon. Sitting beneath a shady piñon, they shared a canteen of already tepid water that Anna had stashed in her small backpack.

Cliff swallows were darting about the massive walls, whizzing by like bullets. Sitting there in the remoteness made Chris feel very cut off from the rest of the world. It wasn't a bad feeling but rather a sensation of timelessness.

"Do you have a lot of friends back home?" Anna asked.

"Not a lot, but a couple real good ones. What about you?"

She shook her head. "No, not many. There's not too many kids around here my age. But at school I have some. That's why summers around here are usually kind of boring."

"Where do you go to school?" Chris asked.

"In Chinle. I have to get up at 5:30 in the morning just to get ready. I have a quick breakfast, then hike to the Ranger's Station, and then catch a bus. Sometimes, when I'm running late, my grandfather gives me a ride."

"Knowing you, that's probably about half the time," Chris teased.

Anna lightly cuffed him on the arm. "Uh-uh. I'm an early riser."

"Your grandmother said you're always in a hurry but seldom on time, remember?"

Anna smiled charmingly. "Well, *sometimes* I am a little late getting there. The teachers seem to be getting used to it, though. Now if they could only get used to Bill showing up and visiting."

Bill heard his name and came over, wagging his tail. He was panting hard so Anna poured some water into her hand and let him lap it up.

"Sometimes I wish I had brothers or sisters," she continued. It would be fun to have a little brother especially. Do you have any brothers or sisters?"

"No. And I'm glad I don't. It would only make things more complicated than they already are."

Anna looked at him inquisitively.

"My mom and dad are getting a divorce," he stammered. "That's sort of the reason I'm out here, I guess. Give them a chance to get everything worked out without a sniveling kid around to get in the way."

"Did they make you come out here?"

"No. It was actually my idea, but they were glad for it. I think they really didn't know what to do with me."

"I'm sorry," Anna said, for once at a loss for words.

"Yeah, me too. It's going to be just great. My dad teaches English at the community college near our house—he'll be moving into an apartment. I'll probably end up seeing him only at Christmas, if I know him. He's going to help Mom with the house payments and other stuff, but she'll still have to go out and get a job. That's a major problem—she's never had an outside job, and I can't imagine what kind of job she'll get. She's an artist, and sometimes she sells one of her paintings, but not often enough to take care of the two of us. I'd sure like to do something to help."

"Maybe you could get a job," Anna offered.

"That's what I think. If I could just find a good job, I'd be able to take care of us. I could work after school and on weekends. Anyway," Chris ruminated as he tossed a stone at a small yucca, "it will work out somehow. It's not like my parents have died or anything."

The comment came out entirely without thought, and Chris instantly wished he hadn't said it. He looked quickly at Anna, wondering what to say.

Anna only nodded and bit her bottom lip. Her eyes stared blankly at the cliff walls in front of her. "Yeah, at least you still have them."

He touched her shoulder gently. "I always seem to say the dumbest things."

"Not really. What you said is true. You need to remember that no matter how bad it gets, it's better than nothing."

She sat with her hands clasped around her blue-jeaned knees, a pensive look on her face. The sun was already low in the sky. In a few hours it would be getting dark.

"Well, should we hike around the other side and then head back? This place is kind of weird, but I don't think it's haunted."

Anna was silent and followed. They each combed different parts of the area, not really sure what they were hoping to find. More pottery shards were scattered about, and here and there lay pieces of agate, a teasing possibility of being an arrowhead.

It was getting late, Chris told himself. Time to head back.

Then Anna suddenly shouted excitedly, "Over here—look!"

Chris ran over.

"Wow!" he gasped, coming to an abrupt stop where Anna stood gaping.

On a large boulder near the base of the cliff were some strange pictures or writings—cryptic images cut into rock. Examining them, Chris could make out what looked like ghost figures—horned, with large hands and feet. Sun and moon shapes circled them, and other symbols, like zigzags and spirals, floated around their heads.

"Unreal!"

"You haven't seen anything yet—get a load of this!" she exclaimed, pointing at another rock.

A cold finger seemed to touch the back of Chris's neck as he turned and stared at their latest find. Something told him this was very significant.

Painted on the rock in front of him, bloodred, were three distinct images; they were faded and worn but still recognizable: a feather, a knife, and a human skull. Each image was about the size of his hand.

"The pictures over there were carved by the Anasazi," Anna pointed out. I've seen enough of their rock art to know. But these images are different—they don't look like any I've ever seen. I'll bet they were painted by the Spanish, or maybe Navajo."

"What do they mean?"

Anna laughed nervously. "How would I know?"

"Wait here," Chris said. "I'm going back to the cycle to get my sketchbook. Maybe somebody back at the lodge will know what they mean if we can show them what they look like."

He returned with his art tools and quickly sketched the images from both rocks. Concentrating on the smallest of details, he figured Anna was probably right. The pictures carved in the rock were carefully and precisely chiseled, whereas the painted feather, knife, and skull looked haphazard and crude, definitely done by a different person at a different time.

It didn't take long to do the drawings. Afterwards, they started back. As they traveled, the reflection from the day's last sun rays sparkled on the cycle's gas tank. The ride was as bouncy and jostling as ever, but Chris hardly noticed. What an incredible sunset, he mused. The clouds looked aflame in the fiery dusk. He was sure that scenes like this would stay with him always. *And now this. Was there a connection between what we heard and saw last night and what we found today?*

Pulling up to the lodge, Chris was surprised to be hailed by Erick.

"Hey, Chris—perfect timing. You're wanted on the phone!"

Knowing who it would be, he ran to the lobby and grabbed the receiver.

"Hello?"

"Hi hon, it's your mom!" came the voice over the crackly line. "Are you having a good time out there? Erick tells me that you've made friends with some little Indian girl. How nice! I do hope you're being careful—especially riding around on motorcycles. I thought Indians rode horses? Listen to me—rattling on. Well, how are you?"

"I'm fine, Mom. I just sent you a postcard. How's everything going with you and Dad?" *Let's hear it,* he thought.

"Well, honey, that's one of the reasons I'm calling . . . your father and I settled everything today; I'm afraid it's final. We don't want you worrying about a thing—you know we both love you. Your father promises he'll be seeing you every other weekend. I know you're concerned about me getting a job—well, I've already lined up some interviews. The job I'm hoping for is a part-time position working in an art gallery. They're also interested in seeing my paintings. You're awfully quiet, dear; can you hear me okay?"

"Yeah, I can hear you fine," he said, wanting to hang up as quickly as possible. "Well, congratulations on the interviews. And thanks for letting me know how things are going. . . . I—I've gotta go . . . bye."

"Bye-bye, hon. I'm really glad you're having such a good time. I can't wait to get your card—I'll write . . . Love you. We've got to hang in there—okay? It's all going to work out. Miss you bunches! Bye, dear."

Hanging up the phone, Chris choked back his impulse to cry. In his peripheral vision, he saw Anna and Erick watching him with long faces. No doubt they knew what was going on. With the taste of tears in his mouth, the flavor of loneliness, he hurried to his room. *What a cop-out. Why couldn't they work things out? Oh sure, at least they were still alive. Yeah, that made him feel so much better!*

Throwing himself on his bed, he began to shut out the world. His eyes burned with tears, but he didn't want to cry. No, he wouldn't cry. He felt bad he'd been so abrupt on the phone with his mom, but what did she expect? What was he supposed to say? *Great, Mom. You and Dad are doing just a great job—messing up our lives!*

A crumpling sound beneath his door forced him to look up. He could see a small, white envelope being stuffed under the door— probably a sympathy note from Erick.

After awhile, Chris went over and picked it up. To his surprise, inside the envelope was the arrowhead Anna had been so thrilled to find. He shook his head, hardly believing it. It felt pretty good right now to have such a friend. *A-n-n-a. Frontwards or backwards it spelled Anna.*

~~~~ *4* ~~~~

MESSAGE ON STONE

I T WAS A DAY AFTER The Phone Call, and Chris was feeling better. Actually, he was surprised by his reaction to the whole thing; he thought he'd prepared himself for his parents' divorce, yet the news had still somehow caught him off guard. It wasn't like he hadn't had time to come to grips with the idea that his parents weren't getting along, that there might be a divorce in the future. No, it wasn't what you'd call a surprise. There had been the telltale signs: the arguments, the mornings of waking up to find Dad camped out in the TV room, or the days of late, when Dad decided not to even bother coming home at all. No, it wasn't a surprise—a shock maybe, but not a surprise.

He spent the day pretty much loafing. Earlier, he had wandered over to the kitchen to show Marie the arrowhead. She, in turn, had navigated him over to the gift shop, where the object of admiration was soon fitted with a clasp so he could wear it as a necklace.

"Hopefully, you won't lose it now," she had said when he thanked her.

He was feeling a little awkward as he anticipated seeing Anna again. How would he break the ice after the phone episode yesterday? Would she, too, be feeling awkward?

These thoughts worried him for most of the afternoon. Finally, when Anna did show up, he realized he'd been fretting for nothing. She noticed the necklace at once and was pleased to see the arrowhead being worn. Her smile said, "Forget it. We're friends and nothing else needs to be said."

Later, they joined Erick for supper in the Thunderbird's cafeteria. His uncle looked sunburnt and tired; evidently he'd had a tough day. Maybe it wasn't the best time to show him the drawings of the rock pictures, but Chris was anxious to get the ranger's opinion. Chris offered to buy Anna supper, which she readily accepted, and they slipped into the booth with Erick.

"Well, to whom do I owe this great honor?" he asked facetiously. "You two have certainly made yourselves scarce around here lately. I was beginning to think you might have run off and eloped or something. Fine. Just ignore me. . . . So what are you gonna do—draw my portrait?"

"We've got some pictures we'd like to show you," Chris explained, opening the sketchbook.

Erick looked at the cryptic drawings while wolfing down large bites of steak. Studying them, he only took his eyes off the paper long enough to locate his glass of milk. Finally looking up, he washed down the last of his meal with a couple of gulps.

"Okay—nice. So you've been drawing the rock art around here; there's definitely a lot of it around."

"We were hoping you might know what it means," Chris answered, already certain they were at a dead end. "I copied these off some rocks in Coyote Canyon."

The mention of Coyote Canyon caused Erick to raise his brow, so Chris explained how they had happened to be out there. Anna interjected occasionally, adding any details that Chris left out.

Erick listened with genuine interest. "Next time you decide on taking a moonlight ride through the canyon on a motorcycle it might be a good idea to let me know about it, don't you think? And yes, you might've discovered something pretty important. It's been awhile since I've been out to those ruins, but I can't recall ever seeing any petroglyphs, or rock art of any kind, in that area. Let's take a ride over there together one of these days so I can check it out, huh?"

"Sure. Do you think these pictures mean anything?" Chris asked.

"Oh, they mean something all right; but if you're asking me *what* they mean, I'm sorry, I can't help you there. You see, the Anasazi made a lot of petroglyphs throughout the whole area. We can only speculate as to their meaning. It's believed that they were carved into the rocks by the shaman—the priest—and were used in magic rituals. Some might've been put there to record events; others could've been made to ensure a good hunt. Who knows."

"Do you think these were made by the Anasazi?" Chris asked, pointing at the three symbols on the opposite page. "Anna says they might've been made by the Navajo."

"I'd tend to agree with her," Erick said. "But I've never seen anything like them before. Most of the Navajo drawings in the canyon depict historical events—battles, astronomical patterns. These look more like a code, a message or something."

Chris closed the sketchbook. *A message or something. What kind of message?*

"Well look, I've got an appointment with a cool shower, so I'll see you around—I hope. Nice necklace, Chris . . . that's some girlfriend you've got," he winked, leaving them both feeling a little embarrassed as he walked off with his tray.

"Hi, kids—may I join you?"

They both looked up to see a thin, small man with a balding head standing at their table. Chris recognized the plaid sports jacket and knew the man was Mr. Reeves, a tourist staying at the Thunderbird.

"I hope I'm not interrupting anything," he said, his amiable smile forcing his mustache to curl up at the ends. "Well, may I?"

Anna just stared, but Chris nodded.

After seating himself, Mr. Reeves plugged a cigarette into his mouth and snapped open a turquoise-covered lighter. "My name's Robert—

Robert Reeves. My friends call me Bob," he confided, still smiling while shaking their hands.

Not wanting to appear impolite, Chris introduced himself. "I'm Chris. And this is Anna."

"Glad to meet you both," he said, exhaling gray smoke. "I don't want to give you the wrong impression, but I couldn't help but overhear the conversation you had with your ranger friend. I hope I don't appear to be an eavesdropper, but the mention of Coyote Canyon certainly pricked my interest. You see, I'm sort of a history buff, interested in just about anything having to do with that intriguing canyon. Matter-of-fact, I'm writing a book. I could use some extra eyes and ears to help me."

Mr. Reeves was so eager to make friends that Chris couldn't help but like him.

"Do you children often play in Coyote Canyon?"

Chris and Anna glanced at each other. *He must think we're about five years old.*

"We were looking for something," Anna said, cautiously.

"Looking for something . . . like ghosts?" he asked, wide-eyed and comically feigning a shudder. "It's haunted, isn't it?"

Chris explained why they had been in Coyote Canyon and what they'd found. Mr. Reeves was very interested, especially in hearing about the pictures on the rocks. Chris felt obliged to show him the drawings.

Mr. Reeves whistled between his teeth. "That's some fine detective work on your part! I guess it means *something.* You wouldn't catch me going in there. No-siree."

A half inch of cigarette smouldered between his index and middle fingers, and when he saw them looking at it, he snubbed it out in the ashtray.

"I appreciate you showing me all this," he said, spilling the last cloud of smoke from his mouth. "If you kids come across anything else, let me know, will ya? With the research I'm doing, I'd be happy to part with a little cash for any out of the ordinary type of info. Oh, by the way—here's soda pop money for later. Don't let the spooks get you."

Dropping a dollar bill on the table, Mr. Reeves sauntered off. Chris said, "Thanks," and followed him out with his eyes. Anna folded the bill and tucked it into her jeans pocket.

"Gas money," she said.

A short time later, the two friends were again combing Coyote Canyon, hoping to find some answers. *What was going on in here the other night? Did it have anything to do with the stories about sheep and cattle disappearing? Did the strange images on the rocks have anything to do with it? If so, what did they mean?*

Climbing among the rocks, Chris was startled by a small fox scurrying out of the underbrush. Bill darted after it pell-mell, but the smaller animal quickly disappeared.

"Did you see that?" Chris cried out.

"Leave it alone, Bill!" Anna yelled. "Or you're gonna get us into some real trouble."

"By chasing a fox?" Chris laughed.

"Navajo tradition has it that if you see a fox, you should either turn around and go back where you came from or wait until four other animals pass you going the other direction. If you don't, you've broken a taboo, and harmony can only be restored by having a medicine man perform a curing ceremony."

Chris shook his head. "You can stand here as long as you want, but I'm not!"

"I said it's a Navajo tradition—I didn't say I always follow it. But then again, I heard of someone who didn't, and . . ."

She walked away nonchalantly, pulling a branch of leaves loose from a tree.

Chris watched her soberly. Anna twirled the leaves in front of her mouth, and he could see she was smiling.

"Yeah. Right. You're . . . " he began and broke off to stare at the leaves. "Wait a minute . . . let's see those leaves. What if the feather that's painted on the rock *isn't* a feather? But a leaf. Like this!"

Anna stared at the leaf he was holding. "It's from this kind of tree," she pointed. "Let's go look at our rock."

A minute later Anna knelt by the painted stone. Chris joined her, contemplating the strange symbols.

"I think it *is* a leaf," he said. "But why paint one on a rock?"

"Maybe it's trying to tell us something about a tree," Anna suggested.

Chris looked around, trying to estimate how many trees with leaves like that were in the canyon. "I once read that Indians buried their dead up in trees. Maybe we'll find a burial site in one of them."

Anna looked at him skeptically. "The Navajo don't bury anyone in trees—and I doubt if the Anasazi did either."

Chris wasn't listening; he was already hiking over to some trees. Anna followed, shaking her head. After looking up the boles of almost every one, Chris was beginning to feel silly. *Okay. Well, nice try. Maybe the picture on the rock is a feather.* Then suddenly something caught his eye. For just a second he thought he'd caught sight of something. Shielding his eyes from the sun, he searched the trunk directly above his head. *What in the world?*

"Anna, come here—look!"

Anna stood next to him, her neck craning as she peered upward. An instant later she grabbed ahold of a low branch and pulled herself up into the tree. Climbing the trunk easily, she made her way up to the thing that was sticking out of the wood. Bill circled below, barking, his tail wagging like a pendulum gone haywire.

Pulling on the object with all her might, Anna barely moved it. She gritted her teeth and continued yanking, pulling harder and harder.

"What is it?" he yelled up at her.

"A knife."

Thinking of the rock drawings, Chris swallowed dryly.

Pulling again with all her strength, Anna suddenly wrenched it free, nearly losing her balance in the process. She then began climbing down.

Chris laughed excitedly. "Hurry up! You're about as graceful up there as a bull elephant."

"I sure hope this knife doesn't slip," she quipped.

Grinning, he stepped out of the way. A moment later she dropped to the ground.

"Let me see it."

She slapped his hand away. "Don't be so grabby. *Yá ah!* Would ya look at this!"

"What? Come on, let me see it!"

Anna reluctantly handed over the knife.

"This is great! I can hardly believe it—it's really old, isn't it?"

She nodded.

"Do you think it belonged to an Anasazi?" he asked, turning the knife over and over in his hand. It had a blade about ten inches long; the metal was rusted and black.

"No, silly, the Indians didn't have steel in those days," she answered.

"I wonder if this means anything?" he asked, showing the knife's handle to Anna.

Carved into the rotted wood was an arrow shape running diagonally, its tail facing the blade and its head pointing toward the hilt. It was faded and barely recognizable. Turning the handle over, they noticed the inscription on both sides.

"It doesn't look like a decoration of any kind," Chris ventured. "It's too crude. It's more like a sign giving directions."

"Right. A *one-way* sign," Anna added, sarcastically. "Traffic control in Coyote Canyon."

Peering up into the tree, he examined the slit where the blade had been. He then surveyed the canyon in the direction facing the trunk wound.

"You know," he said, "when the knife's in the tree, the arrow on the handle would be pointing over there."

"You're right," Anna agreed. "But you're pointing way too high. Remember, this tree, which is a poplar, I think, probably grew a lot since the time this knife was stuck in it—who knows how long ago. The knife looks really old, and I know that these trees live to be ancient—a hundred years or older."

"Brilliant, my dear Watson. Come on, let's follow the arrow and see where it's pointing."

Anna took the lead as they scrambled over rocks and brambles, making their way closer to the canyon wall. With the sun to their backs, Chris noticed that their shadows were stretching longer. It would soon be time to head back again. They might have to wait till another day of investigating to find out if the arrow really meant anything. Besides, they had certainly found plenty to think about today. He wondered if the knife was an antique. The thought of selling it came and went. Some things were simply worth more than money.

Anna was carrying the knife while they climbed around. From behind, Chris thought she looked like some wild warrior of the past; her long, black hair whipped around in a fury as she clutched the big knife.

They had now reached the cliff wall but saw nothing unusual. Chris began searching for possible toe- and handholds niched into the side of the cliff. Then Anna abruptly stopped and stood transfixed, staring at the rock in front of her.

Chris followed her gaze, somehow knowing they had found what the arrow had been pointing at.

A shiver crept up his spine. This proved that the mysterious images *did* mean something. First, there was the poplar leaf which had led to the knife; and now the knife had led them to this. Glaring directly at him was a human skull.

Hollowed eyes stared without seeing. Mounted on a shelf in the rock, the skull grimaced at them from about chest height. With sweaty palms Chris reached out to touch it. Anna stepped back. *Jeez, could this be real?* he wondered.

After touching it, he felt a little braver. Brave enough to study it closer. The skull was crusty and chalky looking. Its lower jawbone was missing. Most of the upper teeth were still there, giving the impression that the death head was leering.

Anna wouldn't go near it. She just stared wide-eyed from a distance. "Another taboo broken," she declared. "You shouldn't touch a human bone; the spirits will get after you. Let's get out of here!"

"Wait. Let me have your backpack."

"You're not going to . . ."

Trying not to think about it too much, he quickly but carefully slipped the skull into the canvas sack, then zipped it tight. It was surprisingly light. *Wait till Erick sees this.*

"Crazy *bilagáana*," Anna gibed, looking at him in shock.

"It will make a nice lamp," he jested. "Come on. Let's get out of here."

For the ride home Anna stowed the old knife in her belt, and Chris wore the pack. "Just don't let it touch me," she commanded.

"Fine."

He had to admit it did feel a bit uncomfortable, just the idea of lugging around someone's head. His imagination didn't help matters—he could almost feel the rotted old teeth chomping at his back at every bump.

Anna called over her shoulder, barely audible over the rattle of the engine. "Look up on your right—see anything?"

He did.

Sunlight reflecting off metal. *Something—someone was up there. Why would anybody be watching us? Metal . . . binoculars or a gun?*

Later, coming out of the canyon, Chris breathed a noticeable sigh of relief. Anna's shoulders slouched, relaxing.

"Well, now you know how it feels to be spied on," he said, trying to make light of the whole weird incident.

"Chris, do me a favor . . ."

"Huh?"

"ZIP IT."

He smiled. "Sure. Some people just can't accept constructive criticism."

"Sorry. I can't hear you . . . ."

~~~~ *5* ~~~~

HIDDEN TREASURE

THAT NIGHT AT DINNER, Chris and Anna told Erick about their latest finds. Much to his uncle's relief, they decided not to uncover their treasures at the table. Erick had made it clear that staring eye to eye with a skull wasn't his idea of how to stimulate a healthy appetite.

"But I'm sure you two are really on to something," he commented. "Is there anything engraved on the blade?"

Looking at each other, they shrugged.

"It's hard to say—the metal is so crusty," Chris replied.

"What about the skull? Anything written on it or marking it?"

Again Chris and Anna looked at each other. They both realized that the latest developments only complicated things. *Who put the knife in the tree? Why was a skull setting on a shelf in the rock? How did a knife and skull tie in with the strange things they saw in Coyote Canyon the other night, if they did at all? And you don't know the whole story, Erick, ol' buckaroo. Someone with a gun (or at least a pair of binocs) seems interested in what we're doing in there, too.* Chris smiled dumbly at the backpack resting on his lap.

"Come on," Erick said, picking up his tray and searching for a bus cart. "I've got an idea."

Five minutes later, the three novice detectives were standing in a large utility room behind the lodge. Chris guessed it was the maintenance crew's workshop. Lights were strewn across the ceiling with heavy extension cords, glaring down on the dark oil stains which patterned the cement floor. Tools hung from old hooks set into the walls. What looked like parts of an air-conditioning unit lay neatly along a large hardwood table.

Shortly, Erick located what he was looking for.

"Here," he said, pouring something from a small can onto a rag, "let me see the knife."

Anna handed it to him, and he turned it over in his hands several times, thoughtfully examining the blade. He then wiped the oil-soaked rag over the tarnished metal and began rubbing the blade furiously. Slowly, Chris could see the black metal turning gray. As the rag took on the tinge of the oxidized metal, the blade actually transformed to a deep silver color.

"Well looky here," Erick exclaimed, flashing the stained but shiny knife in front of their eyes. "I think we've found something."

Chris and Anna both bent over the old knife and examined the polished steel. In small but decipherable letters, an inscription was stamped into the metal: CH1.N.M.V.

Casting a questioning glance at his uncle, Chris asked: "Do you know what it means?"

Erick answered with a shake of his head. "Nope. But I'll clue you in on this—I'm certainly going to find out. I think we should plan on a trip down to Tucson to do a little research. The university over there has a wonderful library, and I'm pretty sure we'd be able to dig up something to shed light on all this."

It sounded like a great idea, and Chris and Anna both agreed to go. Of course, Anna would first need to get permission from her grandparents.

"Now let's see the other little goody you've got stashed in there."

Chris dug into the pack and pulled out the skull, its weight feeling heavier all the time. His uncle examined it closely, whistling softly between his teeth.

"This would definitely be considered an anthropological discovery. You two have really outdone yourselves on this one. I think we'll need to turn this baby over to the experts. When that happens, Coyote Canyon will probably be crawling with archaeologists."

"Can I keep it until then?" Chris asked.

"You found it, so I don't see why not. But take good care of it. Well, I can't make out any distinct markings anywhere. This crack on the forehead could be either deterioration or a head wound, but that's just guessing. I wouldn't leave it out where the cleaning maid will see it—that might not give the most positive impression of my funky nephew."

They thanked him for his help, and Erick turned off the lights and started to lock up. Anna would have to be going home soon, but first came the business of stashing the knife and skull. Chris wondered if having a skeleton head for a roommate would have any adverse effects on his sleep. *Dear Mom, Doing fine. Oh yeah, almost forgot to mention—you should see the skull I found. Cute little guy . . . will make a cool lamp. Right now, I'm keeping him in the drawer next to my socks and underwear. But don't worry! Everything's going fine. Not much different around here than back in Minnesota, except for a haunted canyon, spirits buzzing around the place, and skinwalkers . . . . For a vacation spot, it's quite . . .*

While walking back to the motel room Chris and Anna nearly ran into a man coming around the corner. They looked up almost too late.

"Excuse me, Mr. Reeves," Chris stammered. "I guess we weren't watching where we were going."

"And where *are* you going, ghost hunting?" Mr. Reeves queried, chuckling softly.

"No, sir. Back to my room. You see, we've found something that could be important. Erick said there probably will be archaeologists crawling all over Coyote Canyon soon, but we still don't know what it all means."

Chris knew he was rambling, but his excitement was getting the best of him. Still smiling, Mr. Reeves looked at him curiously.

"Is it a secret, or can you kids tell a bored old tourist about it?"

Chris sensed Anna's hesitancy, but he saw no harm in showing him. Unzipping the bag, he pulled out the skull and held it up to an interested Mr. Reeves.

"We deciphered the clues we had shown you and found this," he said.

Mr. Reeves looked at the skull and then at the two sleuths. Chris smiled up into his appraising eyes, happy with their detective work so far.

"You deserve to be very proud of yourselves," Mr. Reeves told them. "You may be helping to unlock answers to great historical questions. Highly commendable, indeed."

Pulling out his wallet, he thumbed through a fat roll of bills. "Detectives of your caliber need financing. I promised to make it worth your while if you kept me informed."

He held out a five dollar bill, but Chris shook his head. "Thanks, Mr. Reeves, but that's okay—we can't take your money. We've just been lucky, that's all. Besides, we're glad to show you the skull. Right, Anna?"

Anna studied her sneakers, kicking at a make-believe stone on the sidewalk. Mr. Reeves ruffled Chris's hair with a hairy hand.

"Thanks, pal. Listen, keep me posted will you?"

"Sure. Goodnight, Mr. Reeves."

Mr. Reeves waved as he stowed his wallet inside his vest pocket and sauntered off.

Back at Chris's room, they dug out their treasures and placed them on the desk. Anna seemed sullen.

"You don't like him, do you?"

Again, Anna studied her shoes. "I don't trust him."

"Why's that?"

She shrugged.

"He's a nice guy, and I'm sure he can tell that you don't like him.

I just don't want to hurt his feelings."

He could sense Anna closing off like the Great Wall of China so he decided to drop it.

"Hey, why don't you take the knife home with you and show it to your grandfather—maybe he'll know something about it."

The idea pleased Anna. She picked it up and tucked it into her belt.

"You can take the skull, too, if you'd like," he said, reaching over to pick it up.

"No. You better keep it here. I'm afraid my grandparents wouldn't be too happy if they knew I was picking up skeleton bones from Coyote Canyon. They'd for sure think I was infected with ghost sickness. Besides, it'll be interesting to hear how well you sleep with this guy staring at you all night long."

"No problem. I'll just see if I've got an extra toothbrush—these teeth would be a dentist's nightmare."

They laughed.

"Actually," Chris continued, "I think this bonehead would make a great beanie. Maybe I can come over wearing it, like this . . . ."

Anna giggled as Chris clowned around, trying to balance the skull on top of his head and walk nonchalantly across the room. It began to slip off, and Chris's expression suddenly turned serious.

"That's it," Anna gibed. "Go ahead and drop it. I'd love to see you explaining to a thousand archaeologists that it was just an accident— fooling around, trying to impress me with your silly . . ."

Just then something dropped from inside the skull's interlacing network of bone, landing with a soft slap on the hardwood floor. Their eyes fell at once to the small object laying near Chris's feet. He immediately picked it up. His fingers trembled. It was leather, dry and as thin as paper, and most of it crumbled apart as soon as he pulled on it. Inside, though, was something even more surprising—a polished rock, like a charm or a piece of jewelry.

They stared in awe at the small, round object that Chris turned over and over in his hand. It was made of green turquoise and some other stone that was black and shiny, and set inside a shell no larger than a nickel. A small hole had been bored into the outer perimeter of the circlet, probably for threading a string through it so it could be worn.

"Wow, a hidden treasure!"

Anna was silent. She picked the object out of Chris's hand and examined it closer. Holding it inches from her nose, she looked like a jeweler inspecting a diamond.

"It's either a type of coin or a piece of jewelry," Chris speculated.

"I think it was worn—like a necklace," Anna said.

"Yeah, an amulet. Can you make anything out of that design? It sort of looks like a bug or something."

Anna smiled. "Not quite, Sherlock. Here, look closer . . . can you see the head and horns? This is his back, like a hunchback; in his hands is a flute. It's a picture you sometimes see carved in the rocks around here. I call it the humpbacked flute player, but I don't know what the Anasazi called it or what it means."

Chris could see it now. It was the side profile of a stick figure with two long antennae-like things sticking out of his head. A bulge stuck out grotesquely on his back. The flute looked more like a long pole stretching all the way from his head to his toes.

"This is really weird. You say you've seen pictures of this guy before?"

"Sure, in certain places. My uncle Kee once told me about him, but I've forgotten most of what he said . . . something about him being real important to the Anasazi."

"What in the world is this thing doing inside a skull?" he wondered aloud.

On Saturday, Chris and Erick set out for Tucson at dawn. The drive would take most of the day, so they planned on spending the night in a hotel and returning on Sunday. To Chris's disappointment, Anna was needed at home for sheepherding and wouldn't be able to join them. Erick said it was just as well, since it would give the two of them a chance to talk privately about some things. Chris knew that the some things would be about his parents' divorce. He really didn't want to talk about it, so he planned on keeping the conversation miles away from the subject.

In his pocket was a Post-it Note with the knife's inscription on it; he had copied it down before handing the knife over to Anna. He also had the amulet with him. After showing it to Erick last night, his uncle had suggested that they bring it along. Maybe they'd be able to dig up something about its origin and meaning.

Arriving in Tucson, Chris had to once again grow accustomed to the traffic and the hustle-bustle of city life. It made him appreciate even more the remoteness and peacefulness of the Navajo Reservation, where there was only about one stoplight every hundred miles.

The university was huge and modern looking, with large palm trees lining the avenue to the library. The place looked almost deserted that midafternoon.

Erick moved about the imposing shelves of books with an adeptness. It wasn't long before a wobbly tower of books stood piled up on a table in a far corner of the history section. Chris felt a little intimidated by the massive volumes of information. It was hard to imagine that anyone actually read books like these. Hours slowly dragged by while Erick buried himself in page after page. Chris helped at first, but later he found himself just wandering aimlessly down the dark, narrow aisles, checking on his uncle periodically.

On one of his passes, he noticed that the high tower of books had now been sorted out into three shorter stacks. Erick looked up and smiled.

"Listen to this, Chris. Says here that the Spanish battled the Navajo in the same area you found the knife back in the early 1800s. After that, the next soldiers to set foot in there were from the U.S. Calvary—Kit Carson's men in 1864. That knife's got to be a hundred years old or more, if it's a day."

"Kit Carson was in Canyon de Chelly? I thought he was some famous frontiersman, like Daniel Boone," Chris queried as he thumbed through a book filled with pictures of the Old West.

"That and a lot more. He was appointed Indian agent by the U.S. government. Both white men and Indians trusted him. Besides being a cunning and resourceful scout, Carson had a reputation for being honest and fair."

Chris looked over at Erick's book to see if there was a picture of the legendary Kit Carson, but there wasn't.

"Hey, buck-o, let's see that inscription you've written down." Erick paused and then said excitedly, "I think we've got it! Listen to this: 'The location of Colonel Carson's camp was near the Canyon del Muerto entrance. Besides the 700 man cavalry, the colonel had mustered another 300 men of the 1st New Mexican Volunteers, Company H. In his final report, Carson noted . . .'"

Chris looked up, puzzled.

"Don't you see—C H 1. N. M. V. must stand for Company H, 1st New Mexican Volunteers.

"It means that the knife you found probably belonged to some guy enlisted in the Carson campaign. What it doesn't explain is what the heck it was doing stuck in a tree. I'd think that it was probably just put there without any rhyme or reason, except we know better. That picture you two deciphered on the rock proves that. Someone actually made a map so that your knife *would* be found—which means they wanted the skull and amulet to be found, too."

Chris nodded in agreement. They seemed to be finding out a lot but not getting anywhere. *What did it all mean? A knife in a tree. A skull hidden in the rocks. And a humpbacked flute player on a medallion—pretty weird!*

They continued searching but were unable to find anything else which could shed light on the mystery. One book did mention something about the humpbacked flute player; it stated that he was known as Kokopelli, an important symbol to the Anasazi. The shaman, or priest, often pecked out images of Kokopelli in the rocks. Speculations as to its meaning ranged from the flute player being a helpful rain deity, to the macabre notion that it was an evil spirit whose hump was a bag full of babies stolen from their mothers.

To complicate things even more, some Navajo even believed that Kokopelli was the trickster, the clown, the Navajo Coyote of lore. To the Navajo, Coyote represented all the improper deeds of mankind.

His ridiculing and satirizing manner symbolized everything outrageous and destructive. Yet this theory was merely speculation also, further confusing the matter.

"Come on, let's hit the road," Erick finally said. "If I don't get out of here soon, I doubt if I'll be able to see straight. As it is, I'll be seeing books in my sleep."

They stepped out of the musty world of information and into the dazzling late afternoon sunlight. A soft breeze blew across the college campus, gently rocking the palms overhead.

Later that night, they checked into a comfortable yet inexpensive hotel near the university. Chris was thrilled that there was a swimming pool, and he promised to make good use of it. With a ghost of a moon already poised overhead, both he and Erick dipped into the cool, thick liquid. A garish green light from the bottom of the pool illuminated and entangled their shadows, creating an almost surreal ending to their day.

Sunday morning activities consisted of packing, running a few errands, picking up supplies, and then heading out Highway 10 toward home. Chris was eager to get back to the reservation.

With one hand resting on the steering wheel and the other combing through his hair, Erick mused: "So what have we got? We've got a knife that belonged to a U. S. soldier from Kit Carson's army, which you found pointing to a skull; we've got a skull, but we don't know who the owner is, or should I say *was*; and we've got an amulet with a humpbacked flute player on it, made by the Anasazi at least eight hundred years ago. This has all come to light since the discovery of some cryptic images, which we assume were painted by the Navajo on a rock in an almost insignificant canyon. Oh yeah, let's not forget the canyon—a canyon that folks less crazy than my nephew claim to be haunted. You add all this up and what have you got? Quite a mystery."

He frowned and adjusted the rearview mirror.

Chris watched the monumental saguaro cacti slipping past his window. Each one was so similar yet so very different. *The answers are hidden in that canyon,* he speculated, chewing on some ambiguous thought.

Miles drifted by. Erick periodically glanced over at his nephew. Chris guessed what was coming next.

"How's everything going with you on the home front—your parents' divorce and everything?"

He shrugged, wishing not to think about it.

"You know, your mom's real special to me—being my older sis. I know you worry about her, but believe me, underneath that gentle exterior is one tough cookie. She'll manage just fine."

Chris was silent.

"If you ever want to talk about it, I want you to feel free to use me as a sounding board . . ."

He imagined he ought to thank his uncle for wanting to be there for him, but he couldn't manage to get a word out. The road wound through breathtaking scenery; the terrain changed from desert to mountain pines as they cut through the outer corner of the White Mountain Apache Reservation.

"I thought people who were married were supposed to love each other," Chris said wistfully.

"They are *supposed to*, but things change, Chris. You're old enough to realize that. No one expects you to understand everything, but sometimes people who once loved each other drift apart. That's what happened with your mom and dad.

It probably started long ago without either one of them even realizing it. But there comes a time after discovering there's a problem when it's either too late to solve it or the effort doesn't seem worth it anymore. I think that's what happened with your folks. It happens all too often. Sure, we could blame your mom and dad, but what good would it do? They're already paying a high price for their mistakes."

Without wanting it to happen, Chris felt hot tears welling up in his eyes as he studied the world outside his window. Erick continued looking over his way, trying to read his nephew's thoughts.

"When people get married, it's supposed to be such a great thing, and then they end up getting divorced and hating each other. I'll never get married, Erick. The whole thing's so stupid. Who needs it, anyway?"

"Well, you might or might not change your mind on that idea. I'm not one to see the world through rose-colored glasses, but I know that marriage can be a good thing, too. It seems to me it would be like an investment—what you put in is what you'll get out, in the long run."

"Do you think I might be able to get a job with you? Mom's going to need more money. I'm a hard worker . . . Mom and Dad both say I am."

Erick smiled and shrugged his shoulders.

"We'll see. I know you're worried about finances, but like I said, your mom's tough, and she's resourceful, too. Let's just wait a bit and see what happens. I think you'd be more of a support to her by continuing to do well in school and by helping out at home, keeping the place straightened up and things like that."

More miles of silence. The conversation didn't help much, Chris sulked. He still thought his parents were to blame for divorcing. He still thought that people who got married *were* being stupid. His grades *were* up. His house chores *were* always done. And there *were* all those empty hours after school and during school breaks that he could put to good use, earning money and helping. Sure, he'd miss out on sports after school, but that wasn't any big deal; it wasn't like he was some big star player. He supposed he could do all right in any sport, if he really wanted to, but he had always had only a mild interest in any of them. He could never get too excited about watching or playing in any game. So there had to be some kind of job he could get.

They pulled into Thunderbird Lodge by midafternoon. Chris helped unload supplies and then jogged over to his room. The trip had been long, and he was glad for the opportunity to stretch his tired muscles. Pulling his key out of his pocket and jiggling it into the keyhole, he was surprised to find the door unlocked. *Unlocked?* Opening quickly, he glanced around the room, relieved to find everything just as he had left it.

DUMB.

It wouldn't have been any fun apologizing to Mr. Murray if anything had been stolen. He promised himself that he'd be more careful in the future; a mistake like that could have cost the lodge some big money, especially if someone had walked off with the TV.

Didn't I lock the door?

Noticing the bed was a little more disheveled than it normally looked, even after he made it, Chris ran across the room and kneeled in front of the dresser. He opened the drawer and threw socks and underwear aside until the bottom of the drawer stared back at him. Empty.

It's not here. The skull is gone . . .

~~~ *6* ~~~

GRANDFATHER'S STORY

T HE TWO FRIENDS SAT atop a large sandstone crag, enjoying the violet afterglow of day. Grayish shadows intertwined with the remaining light, fighting for dominance, while Chris and Anna kept watch over the sheep. Somewhere on the ridge above a crow cawed repetitively, sounding slightly lunatic.

"Maybe the spirits have reclaimed it," Anna said.

"Well, that's one possibility. The other, more realistic, possibility is that someone stole it."

"How would anyone be able to get into your room?" she asked.

"Easy. There's an extra key in the drawer right behind the lobby desk. Someone could've sneaked back there while Murray was away, which is often enough. You know how he is . . . always off doing something."

"But who would want to steal a skull? Better yet, *why* would anyone want to steal it?"

Chris stood up to stretch. "I don't know. But I do know that the only ones who knew about it were Erick and Mr. Reeves."

"You're forgetting about whoever was watching us from up on the cliff. He could've seen everything from up there."

"How do you know it was a *he?*"

Anna shrugged. "Just guessing."

Night was approaching. Chris and Anna worked their way down a tire-rutted trail that led back to the Charleys' hogan. Bill immediately sprang into action rounding up the beleaguered sheep; their baleful looks and bleating cries protested the dog's eagerness to get things moving. A harsh clanging bell announced the whereabouts of Jarvis, the lead sheep, and soon the whole herd was following him home.

"Did you show your grandfather the knife yet?"

Anna shook her head. "No. I didn't think my grandparents would be too happy if they knew where we found it, so I thought I'd wait until you were back. Actually, I was hoping you'd find out enough in the meantime that I wouldn't have to ask him. And I can't help but think that maybe we shouldn't have taken any of that stuff out of Coyote Canyon in the first place; or maybe we should've at least put the skull back, so we don't disturb the *chindi*."

"Just tell your grandfather that we found the knife in a tree," Chris offered, shrugging off her concerns. "And that my uncle found out the rest—about Kit Carson and everything. We don't have to tell your grandfather about the other stuff, but I still think we should show him the knife. Do you think he'll know anything about the battle with Kit Carson's men?"

Anna looked indignant. "Of course he will. I've told you, he's a medicine man. He knows everything about the *Diné*."

"I stand corrected."

Anna returned to her naturally taciturn self. In the growing darkness they walked on for awhile in silence.

"You know, it's really great to be back on the reservation. This place has a way of growing on you—it's so quiet and free from the hectic pace of city life. There aren't any traffic jams or smog or anything."

"Yeah," Anna said. "Nothing harmful around here except haunted canyons, restless spirits, and skulls that get up and walk away, not

to mention some nut up in the rocks with a bad case of nosiness."
She smiled, then bent down and affectionately frisked Bill's matted
fur. "But I know what you mean. I could never leave here, not for
long anyway."

"You want to live here for the rest of your life?"

She nodded. "Forever."

"That's sort of a long time," Chris bemused.

"Oh, I want to travel places someday. I want to go to France, and
I'd love to see Japan . . . gardens and beautiful flowers everywhere.
I'll go to college when I'm eighteen. I could see a lot of places and
then come back here to live."

"What would you do when you come back? I'll bet there's not a
great demand for Navajo princesses these days."

She tried to give him a scathing look. "Ha—ha."

He laughed.

Ignoring him, Anna said matter-of-factly, "My uncle Kee says our
people are destroying the land by overgrazing their sheep on it. He
says they need to be taught soil conservation and ecology. I think I
would be a good teacher, so—who knows? I just know that I want to
protect this land."

Chris listened attentively. He could picture Anna being someone
important someday. *Actually, she already is pretty important,* he thought.

"Well, when I'm a rich and famous artist, I'll have to come back
here and do a commission job for the Navajo conservation special-
ist Miss Anna Joe. You know, I'll paint great murals of Canyon de
Chelly all over the country, promoting your cause."

"Gee, that would be swell, Chris," Anna said with mock enthusiasm.
And don't forget, you could sign each one with 'Missing: lovely skull
with winning smile. Last seen in my motel room next to my socks
and undies. If you have any information on the whereabouts of this
guy, please contact C. W., famous artist.' "

They both laughed as they came to an old wooden pen just as the
first stars appeared. Bill herded the sheep inside in no time; they closed
the gate, and their work was finished. Chris could see Arletta lighting
a kerosene lantern near the door of the Charleys' hogan. Earlier that

day, he had been invited to spend the night, and Erick had consented. So now Chris and Anna both stopped to wash their hands in a bucket of cold, soapy water before entering the hogan for dinner.

Chris noticed right away that Davidson Charley wasn't around, and he wondered if they would miss their chance to talk to him. Chris ate his mutton stew mostly in silence, intermittently muttering, *"ahyeh eh,*—thank you," or *"shil likan,"* meaning "tasty."

Pots and utensils were later stowed away while Anna and her grandmother chatted in Navajo. Occasionally, Chris felt they were talking about him, and their giggling made him feel even more self-conscious. Finally, Anna turned and smiled.

"My grandmother likes you."

"That's just great. Maybe I can hire myself out as the local entertainment around here. I seem to be pretty funny without even trying."

"Oh, Chris, you're so grumpy sometimes."

He was just about to remind her of who was usually the grumpy one when she added, "We were just talking about how cute you are."

Chris could feel his ears growing warm, and Anna laughed at the sight of his blushing. The situation wasn't getting any better.

Finally, Anna threw a heavy wool blanket over her shoulders and stood near the door to leave. Chris followed, accepting the blanket handed to him by Arletta. The old Navajo woman fussed with Anna's blanket as they filed out, the way grandmothers worry themselves over a granddaughter. The night air had turned frigid, making Chris all the more appreciative of the blanket.

"Where are we going?"

"My grandfather's been out all day gathering herbs for medicine. He's probably just finishing with his prayers now, so it'll be a good time to talk to him. There he is over there."

Chris could make out the glare of a fire among the rocks nearby. A shadowy figure was seated in the incandescent hollow, slowly rocking back and forth, his shadow looming above the orange glow on the rocks. Walking over to the old medicine man, they quietly sat down and listened to his soft chanting.

Kindling wood snapped, and sparks drifted up into the night like small flickering fireflies. A sweet, smoky aroma filled Chris's nostrils; it was the smell of burning juniper, the perfumed scent of hot resin. A murky waft of air swept around the sandstone cranny, whipping up an eerie howl which further teased his senses. He shivered. Davidson Charley continued staring into the flames as though he were hypnotized, his singing growing fainter and fainter.

After awhile, Anna gently touched her grandfather's shoulder. The old man looked up.

"Grandfather, we share in your prayers, and we desire to walk in beauty."

The medicine man looked into his granddaughter's young face and smiled, his wrinkles deepening like cracked leather. He nodded and clasped her small hand.

"What is it you want, child?"

Anna drew out the knife from under her blanket and said, "We found this, Grandfather. We know that it belonged to one of Kit Carson's soldiers—it's written here. But there are stories about this knife that are hidden. You see, it was stuck in a tree, and we think it was put there for a reason. Maybe if we knew more about the soldiers and the battle with our people, we might know what story the knife holds."

The old man's gnarled hand held the blade over the fire. Time seemed to stand still while he meditated over the glowing metal.

Finally, he handed her back the knife and said: "There are stories about the battles in the canyon . . . many stories. They run like vessels into one great artery. The artery flows into our river of blood known as The Long Walk."

"Could you tell us the story, Grandfather?"

Again the firewood crackled, and a flurry of sparks popped into the blackness. Hungry flames licked the air. More time elapsed, making it impossible to determine the hour. Chris began seeing macabre faces dancing among the glimmering cinders.

Davidson Charley began his story in a soft, melodious voice, revealing a deep empathy with the unforgotten years. Firelight reflected off his eyes as he stared into the burning inferno of the past.

"We came to the canyon hundreds of years ago. We learned from the Ancient Ones. We learned how to plant corn and beans and how to harvest. There was harmony with our neighbors as we settled into the rhythms of this land."

He stoked the fire with a juniper log. "General Carlton saw the *Diné* as a great problem; our people often raided the settlers who came here, stealing sheep and cattle. Sometimes people got killed. Carlton asked the great scout and pony soldier Kit Carson to come and defeat us—to send us to Bosque Redondo. We had fought the Spaniards for many years, and now we had to fight the U.S. Cavalry."

"What is Bosque Redondo?" Chris asked.

"Prison camps in New Mexico," the medicine man answered. "Kit Carson brought a thousand soldiers into our sacred canyon to fight us. The *Diné* hid in the rocks and were hard to find. Some were never found. Others joined the Apaches in the south. As the soldiers looked for us, they burned our crops and fruit trees."

Davidson Charley paused and looked into the glowing embers. Chris began to wonder if he had finished, but he abruptly began his tale again.

"It was early in January when Carson's troops arrived for battle. Deep snow covered the ground, and it was bitter cold. In the first skirmish, eleven warriors were killed—soon, many more. There were few guns and little food among our people. They were sick and starving. It wasn't much of a fight. The *Diné* surrendered soon after."

"That was it?" Chris asked.

"That was the beginning. Thousands of *Diné* lost their will to fight when they saw their sacred canyon invaded. To see enemies victorious in their Canyon de Chelly was too much to bear.

"Thousands of *Diné* were rounded up and ordered to walk to Bosque Redondo. We call it The Long Walk. Many died along the way. Others were dragged away to be slaves; children were many times separated from their parents. Those who got to the camps were welcomed with starvation and disease—more died. Finally, after four years of hardships, it was all called a *mistake*. They sent the *Diné* home—those who were left."

"Why didn't more people run away when the soldiers came?" Chris asked. "They would've never found them with all the places around here to hide."

A sad smile from the old man acknowledged him. "Many did hide, and they died from the cold or from starvation. The temptation to stop one's hunger is great. The *Diné* who surrendered were promised food and clothing; usually it never came, of course."

The flames died down to luminous coals, and Chris at once felt the chill. Davidson Charley showed no intent to rekindle the fire.

"It is said that there were some who did escape, but this is not certain. There are old stories about a hiding place—a place of magic provided to us by our ancient friends—but who can say. Many stories are woven by the imagination."

Ancient friends? Chris pondered. *The Navajo were provided a magic hiding place by their ancient friends? But that would be the Anasazi; and they disappeared from here hundreds of years before the Navajo even arrived in the canyon. Is he talking about ghosts?*

Chris wanted to ply Davidson Charley with more questions, especially about the magic hiding place, but he sensed better. The story was over.

Later that night, he took his place on the floor inside the Charleys' hogan. He unrolled the sheepskin blankets and slipped inside with his clothes still on. Somewhere in the darkness to his left was Anna; Arletta and Davidson Charley were at the other end of the small dwelling. He could hear them talking softly in Navajo and wondered what they were saying.

Lying there, his eyes grew accustomed to the darkness, but he dared not look around. In fact, the temptation to even shift his weight was stifled, since he was afraid of making too much commotion in such close quarters. He thought about the many baffling parts of their mystery. The only thing he knew for sure was that the knife was connected to the battle which took place between Carson's soldiers and a famished band of Navajo. The connection between the knife and the Anasazi amulet wasn't clear.

An idea tugged at the back corridors of his mind but gently eluded him. He was nagged by a feeling that he was overlooking something, or that he was making some sort of mistake. He yawned. Sleep soon spun its web, seizing his thoughts and weaving them into irrational strands of dreams. The dreams teased his worries, and then they disappeared.

A cock crowing at the gray of dawn was his alarm clock. Chris took a brisk walk to the outhouse, where a basin of cold water near the door revived him. Even though he thought he had risen early, he found that he was the last one up and just in time for breakfast.

After a meal of fry bread, eggs, and bacon, he was driven back to the lodge in Davidson Charley's old pickup. Riding in the back with Anna and her dog, he bathed in the warmth of the morning sun as they bumped along their way. Today, Anna would be visiting relatives with her grandparents, so Chris would be on his own. When they stopped in front of the Thunderbird, he jumped out and waved good-bye. Anna waved back, and Bill barked farewell as the truck labored grumpily down the road.

Walking toward his room, Chris began planning his day. Since his letter writing hadn't fared well lately, it would be a good project to start, he thought.

Mr. Reeves stood near his door, and Chris smiled and said, "Good morning."

"Good morning, sport. So how's our young Casanova?" he said with a wink.

Not understanding the gibe, he smiled and responded, "Fine."

"You know," Mr. Reeves continued, "when I was your age I wouldn't have dared pull the shenanigans you're pulling. . . . A word from the wise—just be careful not to get in over your head!"

Another wink.

Chris's expression must have shown his bewilderment.

"Don't play dumb with me, my young friend. I have eyes, and I wasn't born yesterday. What you do with your life is your business. Just don't do anything I wouldn't do, which leaves you wide open! Ha—ha."

"I'm sorry, Mr. Reeves, but I don't have any idea what you're talking about."

"Uh-huh. Don't know what I'm talking about, eh? Come on! I saw her myself. But it's really none of my business."

"Saw who?"

"Who? That cute little girlfriend of yours, who else? Last Saturday night I saw her slipping out. Must've been after midnight. I wasn't trying to be snoopy or anything, just couldn't sleep and I thought I heard something. And there she was—sneaking out of your room like a little nymph. I could see it was her even though you had all your lights off; it was a pretty bright night."

Chris stood with his mouth wide open, not knowing what to say. Saturday night he had been in Tucson with Erick.

Suddenly a cold light illuminated his brain. *Maybe we should've at least put the skull back, so we don't disturb the* chindi. *Wasn't that what she had said?* He walked away from Mr. Reeves, who was still droning on. *That's it. Anna stole it. She broke right into my room and stole the skull!*

~~~~ *7* ~~~~

BILL SEES TROUBLE

Bill was restless.

On the prowl, the dog had covered miles of canyon in the past few hours. He stopped occasionally, sniffing at the kaleidoscope of scents being carried through the fronds of tamarisk. Sometimes the windward fragrances were enticing enough to investigate, especially if they indicated the presence of a jackrabbit or desert mouse. Sometimes the wind only held the scent of dried snakeweed or greasewood. Nevertheless, Bill roamed through the numerous arroyos and small washes, unintentionally drifting closer and closer to the entrance of Coyote Canyon.

A sliver of a moon waned in the sky, barely high enough to cast its pale light on the cliff walls. The night was at its darkest, the graveyard hours just before dawn. Bill stopped and peered into Coyote Canyon. Scratching with a hind paw, he instinctively sensed the presence of danger. His tongue lolled out of his mouth, licking his

nose and upper jowl in one unpretentious sweep. Looking forward, then backward, then forward again, he worried about his next move.

For five years Bill had enjoyed the complete freedom of wandering where he pleased, when he pleased. He knew most of the tributaries known as Canyon de Chelly better than anyone. He had eagerly explored most of the canyon at one time or another, either at Anna's side herding sheep or during the night hours. Few crannies had escaped his curiosity.

But tonight was different. Tonight, an observer would have noticed that the dog looked worried. He trotted onward, sensed something distressing, yet cautiously probed deeper into the quiet ravine. Somewhere in the night, a crow screeched. Bill pricked his ears, whined deep within his throat, and started off toward the nocturnal sound. Something was wrong. Very wrong. Many miles away, Anna tossed in her sleep.

Bill had always shied away from this particular place. The only times he had ventured into Coyote Canyon were with Anna and Chris. He had felt safe with Anna. It was always safe with Anna. Ever since he had been a pup, she had cared for him—fed him, loved him. He had been her surprise gift presented in a beautifully wrapped box on her seventh birthday. And now he was one of Anna's only ties with her deceased parents.

It was love at first sight for Anna and the puppy. Anna's parents had decided that Bill would stay at the Charleys' hogan to help with the sheep, and Anna would walk the short distance from her home to take care of her dog. Through the years, she gladly fulfilled her responsibilities in caring for her pet, and their bond became unbreakable. After the death of her parents, the two became inseparable. "If there's a negative aspect to this relationship," Anna's grandparents had heard from her sixth grade teacher, "it's that Anna has withdrawn from most of her peers and finds solace only with an animal." Being a traditional Navajo, Davidson Charley believed that the Beauty Way would heal in ways that happen without outside manipulation—that Anna would be healed without interference from teachers or others. *Hozho*, perfect harmony, perfect peace, would be attained gradually through the ceremonies taught by Changing Woman and the other Holy People. Being a medicine man, Davidson Charley had recited many of these chants over his granddaughter himself, and had witnessed a gradual healing.

Bill was now at the far end of the box canyon, an area dotted with tamarisk, wild asters, and cheat grass. Tumbled walls from another age perched on a shelf pressed into the deepest hollow in the rock. A shroud of stillness covered the ravine. It was too quiet. Quiet like the dead.

Suddenly, out of a crack in the darkness Bill heard the wild flutter of wings. A shadow in the night passed overhead, landing on a solitary pinnacle of sandstone.

A crow.

The huge bird was perched as a sentinel atop the petrified minaret, looking ominous. Bill's hair stood straight up on his hunched shoulders. A low growl ignited in his stomach, venting its way up his throat and out between bared teeth. He sensed something threatening here, something life threatening.

"CAAWWWW."

The crow's raucous scream shattered the last remnants of night. "CAAWWW. CAAWWWW."

Its screech, as unnerving as the pulling of an old, rusty nail, penetrated deep into Bill's heart. With his tail tucked between his legs, he ducked into a nearby cul-de-sac.

The crow glowered down at him with eyes burning like flushed embers, its long, wicked beak opening and closing, opening and closing. Bill peeked out; the bird hissed.

Suddenly it vanished.

The stone pinnacle seemed to totter. Solid stone transformed into thick liquid, rippling like a dark, disturbed pool, turning translucent. Massive rock evolved into some kind of human mutation; a monstrous figure of a man, towering and gaunt, emerged.

Shrouded in a cloak, the thing swayed like a reeling giant. Its face was ancient, but of flesh and bone. Its sunken eyes were closed. Thick strands of rope-like hair fell onto straight, broad shoulders.

An angry gust of wind kicked up at the base of the human apparition, throwing sand and debris into a small cyclone, splitting the heavy
stillness. The colossus began to shudder. Its eyelids flew open, revealing
wide, empty sockets. Mummified lips drew back tightly, grinning. Bill
bolted. With a final look back, he saw wrinkles racing across the face,
deepening and cracking. It was still grinning as the flesh peeled away.
Bill ran like the wind.

The night also fled, and morning found the courage to exert itself.
Anna awakened, dressed, and looked around for her dog. Bill was still
sleeping. Later, she would take him with her as she rode over to
see Chris.

PART II

Secrets of the Present

~~~ *8* ~~~

CHRIS SEES THE LIGHT

Chris's Room, 10:15 A.M.

FLATTENING THE CRISP GRASS struggling to survive, a sudden gust blew across Thunderbird Lodge. Chris wandered over to the picture window and tugged the drawstring of the curtain, allowing morning light to flood the room. Feeling anxious about having to confront Anna, he punched the button on the TV set and plopped down on his bed. She would be here any minute, and he wasn't sure what he'd say to her. He hated confrontations. *As the World Turns* was just going on a station break. He stood up and turned it off. The soap was one that his mother never missed, not until now anyway. His dad had often chided her about watching it, calling her a couch potato, or the stereotypical bored housewife. Thinking of her, he glanced at the typewriter he'd borrowed from Erick. *Time to get a letter off.*

Pulling the wobbly desk over to the edge of the bed, he loaded the typewriter with paper and started pecking:

Dear Mom:

How's everYthing going in the Twin Cities? I'm doinhg just fine.

Sorry I haven't written sooner—just lazy I vguess. Erick let me use his typewriter, but the trouble is there's no correction tape, so I apologize for amy mistakes. How's the job hunt going? A ny luck?

I've been having a great time, mostly. Erick is at some meeting in Flagstaff today. I guess it came up all of a sudden. We had planned on a horseback trip into the canyon, camrping out under the stars. Erick's friend Kee and a friend of mine (*was she anymore?*) were syupposed to go with us. Oh well, I'm sure we'll do it later. Well, sivnig ioff for now. See you later.

Love,
Chris

It was short, but it would do. Lately, he had found it more and more difficult to communicate with her. To *really* communicate. She seemed distant, preoccupied. But then again, maybe he wasn't doing such a fine job communicating either. Didn't *listening* have something to do with communication? When was the last time he asked her how *she* was doing, how *her* day was? Mom, the Great Pillar of Security, maybe needed a listening ear once in awhile, or a compliment out of the blue. The thought suddenly struck Chris that maybe adults weren't *that* different from kids, just bigger, that's all, with more responsibilities. Maybe they still got scared sometimes, still felt unsure of themselves once in awhile. Maybe they, too, still needed encouragement, needed someone to understand them, to love them. It was a heavy-duty thought.

Pushing the desk away, he was beginning his search for an envelope when a knock sounded on the door. *Anna.* He felt a tightening in his stomach as he reached for the doorknob.

Wearing faded jeans and a red and white checkered blouse, she was standing there with her shadow puddled at her heels. The first thing he'd have to do, he thought, was let her know that the camping trip had been scratched.

"Hi!" she greeted.

"Hi. Uh, come in."

"Boy, I thought I was gonna be late. My grandfather saddled Pepper for me, and my grandmother packed me so much food that I could feed all of us for a week. Bill, stay out!

"I couldn't find that silly dog anywhere this morning. I swear, he's been acting so strange all day. I finally found him snuggled up with the lambs, just like he used to do as a pup . . . what's the matter?"

"Uh, nothing. Erick's not here. Won't be back until tomorrow. So I guess our camping trip's been canceled."

"Oh."

Anna sensed the tension. "Do you wanna go riding or anything?" she asked, still trying to smile. "I'll let you ride Pepper, and I'll ride the stable horse you were going to rent."

"I don't think so. I've got tons of letters to write."

"Okay. Well, um, guess I'd better go help with the sheep today . . . sorry to interrupt," she said, trying not to look hurt. "Come on, Bill."

"Anna, wait a minute—I know who stole the skull."

She turned her head so quickly that her ponytail whipped from one side to the other.

"You do?"

"Uh-huh. And so do you."

She frowned.

"You don't know what I'm talking about?"

"Fraid not."

"Oh come on, Anna! I know you took it. I don't know why you didn't just tell me that you thought you should return it, if that's what you did. There was no reason to steal it out of my room."

Anna shook her head. "You're loco," she snapped. "What makes you think I stole it?"

"I've got my sources. Please, just fess up, all right?"

"Crazy *bilagáana*. You have no right accusing me."

"Oh. Forgive me, Your Highness. Who am I to question the great Navajo princess? If she wants to break into my room, that's her royal privilege!"

She stared at him. Her dark eyes were potent fires. Her wide mouth was set. "I didn't know you were such a jerk."

"Well, I *knew* you were weird, but I didn't think you'd . . ."

"I don't want to talk to you anymore," she said, scowling toughly at him through glassy eyes. She turned and started walking away. A few seconds later she ran.

Chris suddenly realized that he was shaking and had been for some time. He balled his hands into fists and felt the shaking move to his stomach. *What a crummy day,* he thought.

Coyote Canyon, 12:00 noon

Anna slowed Pepper to a walk. The paint snorted and pulled against the reins, still wanting to run.

"Take 'er easy, girl. You need to rest."

Rubbing her hand over the coarse, wet, horse hair, Anna patted the mare's neck. She was a skilled enough rider to know how far she could push her mount and when to let up. She also knew it was best to rest a tired horse by walking it, rather than coming to a full stop. They had ridden hard, and Anna was feeling better now. She knew what she had to do.

Stopping only once to sniff at an inquisitive lizard that peeked out from beneath a rock, Bill tagged along close behind. Anna glanced up at the sky; a lone thunderhead drifted above. The cloud would be visible for a hundred miles in every direction. She didn't like being in this canyon, especially alone, but there was no other way. Her grandfather had taught her that she should try to stay in harmony with all things; getting involved in matters that didn't concern her would disrupt the natural order.

Now she would restore the harmony. She would return the knife that she had taken to its rightful owner. She would give it back to the tree. She never wanted to see Chris again, but maybe this would help the hurt go away. Maybe she could forget all this business about unraveling mysteries.

After finding the tree and digging the knife out of her well-stocked saddlebags, she was able to replace it without any difficulty. Feeling relieved, she climbed out of the old poplar.

Several thick, round-topped cumulus clouds had gathered together by now. Their hazy outline promised an eventual thunderstorm. Anna looked around, suddenly aware of the loneliness that surrounded her, and the danger. She looked up at the old ruins. *Houses of the dead,* she thought. *Many chindi have found freedom from their bodies around here.* Her grandfather had told her about the *chindi,* the ghost that is in every living thing. After the body dies, it passes from the shell that contained it and dwells nearby, waiting to cause harm or death to the living. To even speak the word *chindi* was dangerous, because one might then come to you. Anna thought about her ghost beads which lay somewhere, forgotten until now, hidden among her belongings. She wished she had brought them for protection.

Pepper neighed impatiently. The wind started to pick up.

"It's okay, girl. We're leaving."

As soon as she mounted, Anna had the uneasy feeling of being watched. Again, she glanced up at the cliff dwellings.

This place gives me the creeps.

"Come on, Pepper!"

As with most accidents, it happened so suddenly there was no time to prepare for it. One moment she was coaxing her mount to a sprint; the next, she was being thrown from the saddle, landing hard on the sunbaked sand.

Dusting sand from her palms, she stood up and concentrated on calming her racing heart. Bill trotted over and offered a comforting lick.

"I'm all right, Bill," she said, petting him behind the ears. "Let's go see how Pepper's doing." Her legs felt shaky as she began to walk.

The horse was standing under a cottonwood, eyeing Anna with distrust. She gently reached for the bridle.

"You all right, girl? What happened to us, uh?"

Her hand barely touched the reins when Pepper jerked her head back and trotted off, stopping a short distance away. Noticing that her horse was limping, Anna swore softly under her breath.

"Come to me, Pepper. Are you angry with me?" she asked while fumbling for a sugar cube in her jeans pocket. "*Na há chíish?*" she asked again, in Navajo. "I'm sorry, girl. Here—let's make up. *T' aadoo ná há chí í í.*"

Pepper slowly limped over to the sugar cube, sniffed it with flared nostrils, and then lipped it out of Anna's palm. Anna lifted the horse's front left leg and felt along the lower shank. *No break,* she thought, relieved. Then Anna studied the canyon; there was a considerable number of Russian olive trees and tamarisks in one of the small arroyos, a sure sign of water seepage. It would be safe to leave her horse here and walk back. She and her grandfather could return later with the pickup and trailer.

"We'll be back for you later, Pepper. There's plenty of water for you over there. Don't be afraid, girl. I'll be back before you know it."

Throwing a last look over her shoulder, Anna began trudging her way out of Coyote Canyon with Bill following. From out of the corner of her eye she saw something move . . . it came from the ruins.

Something.

Is somebody up there? She turned, shielding her hand over her eyes, studying the ancient stones. Again, she saw movement. *There's something in there!*

An animal.

Something.

Anna spun around to run but stopped dead in her tracks, too terrified to move. Bill growled. Fear crept into her face as she stared at the menacing figure standing in front of her.

Thunderbird Restaurant, 5:20 p.m.

"I thought you were off on an overnight in the canyon," Mr. Murray remarked, sitting down across from Chris. "Where's that crazy uncle of yours?"

Chris explained about the change of plans for the second time that day. "I guess we'll probably reschedule it when . . ."

"Murray, did you ever order those butter patties like you said you were gonna?" Marie flopped down next to Chris, shaking the table and throwing him a smile. "Hi, hon. Where's that pretty little girlfriend of yours?"

"What butter patties?"

"She's not my *girlfriend*."

"What butter patties?" Marie gibed. "The ones you said you were gonna order last weekend. Did you forget? I'll bet you forgot. Good grief, Murray, we'll have to use margarine blocks."

"No, no, you're not going to have to do no such thing! They've been ordered. Matter-of-fact, Sadie told me she ordered some. Yeah, I forgot, but her order oughta be coming anytime. So I forgot—I can't remember everything around here!"

"I knew it!" Marie exclaimed, actually sounding happy about it. "I *knew* you forgot. I'll go get the margarine out."

Marie bounced up, almost colliding with Kee as he stood holding a tray stacked high with mutton and fry bread.

"May I join you?"

Mr. Murray swatted the air. "Arrest that woman for me, Kee. She's too good of a cook for me to fire her, so you've got to arrest her. It's the only way I can be rid of her."

Kee looked at Chris, and they both smiled. The Navajo ranger slid into the vacated seat next to him.

"You look tired," Mr. Murray noted.

"I am. Speaking of arresting someone, that's just what I'd like to do."

Mr. Murray raised an inquisitive brow. Chris looked up from his plate of cold fries and half-eaten cheeseburger.

"We found some ruins in Canyon del Muerto that were just recently robbed—a real clean job. The work of professionals," Kee said.

"Professionals?" Chris asked.

"Professional pothunters," Mr. Murray explained. "Thieves. They'll go into a site that archaeologists haven't touched yet and tear the place apart. Sometimes they'll even go in with a backhoe, if they can get it into the area."

Chris looked puzzled. Kee explained further: "You see, these guys will go into ruins that archaeologists are saving for later digs. They get in there first and dig up all the ancient pots, then sell them— usually back East. There are collectors in places like New York who'll pay thousands of dollars for a single pot."

Mr. Murray pulled an old pipe from his shirt pocket, hit it against his palm several times, and then struck a match.

"Any idea who's doing it?" he asked, holding the pipe stem between his teeth. His corner of the table was already half engulfed in smoke.

"Not a clue. They're real good, these guys. They must've made off with quite a haul, and we haven't the slightest idea how they got in or out of there without being seen."

"What'll happen to them if you catch 'em?" Chris asked. "Will they go to jail?"

"They'll go to jail all right. Pothunting's a violation against the Federal Antiquities Act. That makes it a felony," Kee commented.

Mr. Murray lit another match and held it to the smoldering tobacco. "You know, it strikes me as peculiar that for the past several years this looting has gone on around the same time of year. Whoever these guys are, I'd bet they're not locals. Local thieves would be plundering all year long, right? These are outsiders."

"Well, that's some good detective work on your part, Murray," Kee said. "You may be right. I'd like you to keep your eyes open and let me know if you see anything that looks suspicious. I'd really like to bag these guys."

"You bet. You taking off, son?" Mr. Murray asked as Chris slid out of the booth.

"Y-yeah. I'll see you later—bye," Chris stammered, trying not to run through the cafeteria with his tray. His head was swimming.

He suddenly *knew* who was plundering the ruins in Canyon del Muerto. He knew who had been spying on Anna and him as they were riding out of Coyote Canyon the other day. He also knew who had really stolen the skull out of his room, though he didn't have the slightest idea *why*.

Now it was his turn. He slipped behind the unattended lobby desk, opened the top drawer, and fished through the loose keys until he found it—the key to room 106. He stuffed it into his pants pocket and walked out.

Once outside, he glanced around casually, relieved there was no one in sight. As he walked down the narrow pathway leading to the rooms, he noticed the heavy clouds gathering over the canyon.

Room 106, 5:45 P.M.

Chris knocked on the door and waited. No answer. The curtains were drawn, making it impossible to see inside. He mustered all of his courage, glanced to the right and left, inserted the key, turned it, opened the door—just enough to slip inside—and closed it. He was in.

This is really dumb, buck-o. What are you going to tell him if he shows up?

Looking back on everything, Chris knew he was right about Reeves. It all seemed so obvious now: his interest in all the things he and Anna had found; his inquisitiveness as to where they had found them; his small bribes; his apparent lie about Anna being in his room, just to take any suspicion off himself; and Anna's intuitive distrust of him. *Mr. Reeves had to be the one who stole the skull. But why? Why would he want it? Had he known that the humpbacked flute player was stashed inside? Did he know why it was in there?*

Chris went to the drawers in the corner of the room and quietly opened them, sifting through the contents. Nothing. Looking around, he spotted some papers inside the undershelf of the night table. Thumbing through them, his heart began to race. Among the papers were several catalogs from auctions of American Indian art. The corners on a number of pages were folded over. Flipping one of the catalogs open, he saw that the dog-eared pages featured illustrations of Anasazi pots. Prices ranged from $4,000 to $50,000. Three of the pots on one page had been circled in red. He put the catalogs back and thumbed through the rest of the materials. Nothing else looked important.

He sat on a corner of the bed, wondering what to do next. He knew he was pushing his luck and that he ought to leave. His eyes wandered over to two photos setting atop Reeves's desk. Both were in cheap, imitation gold frames; both looked out of place in the impersonal setting of a motel room. He looked closer. The smaller one was a picture of a woman, older than his own mother, yet younger looking than Mr. Reeves. *Is it Mrs. Reeves?* he wondered. She looked kind of sickly. Her large eyes looked sad and tired, her face drawn. He reached over to the other photo. A war picture, five men grinning into the camera. They were all wearing leather flight jackets, their cloth caps cocked insolently on their heads. In the background was a military helicopter with the name MAGPIE scrawled across the nose. Flipping the photo over, Chris read the caption at the bottom: "U.S. Marines, 9th Division, Airborne—S. Vietnam, October 14, 1965." Looking at the photo again, he studied the men closer. His eyes kept returning to a young man with a pencil-thin mustache who was smiling recklessly. Mr. Reeves.

Mr. Reeves the Vietnam War vet. Mr. Reeves the husband. Mr. Reeves the friendly tourist. Mr. Reeves the pothunter, the thief, the liar.

Chris rubbed his forehead and tried to think. His entire body crawled with a mixture of fear and excitement. He could feel the hair stirring on the nape of his neck.

Outside, a muffled cough and a rattle of keys caught Chris's attention. He heard the unmistakable sound of a key being inserted into a lock. The lock on room 106.

∿∿∿ *9* ∿∿∿

WAKING THE DEAD

"THERE'S NOTHING ELSE we can do," Mr. Reeves argued. He was standing in the doorway. "But we better move quickly and carefully. Leave the unexpected cargo to me—I'll take care of it. *Accidents* happen, right?"

"I don't know. I don't like it . . . nobody's s'posed to get hurt, r'member?" an unfamiliar voice said.

"For cripes sake, Arnie, don't go gah-gah on me! I didn't plan on this happening any more than you did. Whad'ya want me to do—call it off?"

Chris was listening to the strained conversation from underneath Reeves's bed. The sudden arrival of the two men had left him with no other choice than to dart under it for cover. His heart raced. Peering out, he could see Mr. Reeves's boots still at the doorway. For the first time in his life he wondered if he might be into something way over his head.

"Listen," Mr. Reeves continued, "just get everything together. It's all under control, okay? Have I been wrong on anything yet? I'm tired. Get over to Hal's and be ready to wake the dead."

The other man grumbled something, and then the door closed. Boots crossed the small room and stopped near the nightstand, inches from Chris's face. His heart was throbbing in his ears. The boots moved. Suddenly, the bed sagged with a squeaking ferocity, the mattress springs quivering just inches from his face. Chris pushed his cheek into the carpet and stared at the boots, trying to calm his breathing.

He's going to hear my breathing! I know he's going to hear my breathing!

One boot lifted off the carpet, a moment passed, and then it landed in the corner with a soft thud. A gray, stockinged foot appeared in its place. Next, the other boot disappeared, another thud, another gray stocking. Chris heard Mr. Reeves mumble something, but he couldn't make out what he was saying. *I'm breathing too loud!* The bedsprings lifted with a creak. Gray socks moved around the room. He could hear drawers open and close, open and close. Something rustled. To his horror, a crumpled piece of paper dropped near his nose. A large, hairy hand appeared, clawing at it. Chris suddenly had to pee very badly.

The gray socks padded off toward the bathroom. A minute later, bathwater was running. Chris heard the pull of the shower curtain and the spray of water. He waited. The spray continued, its condensation escaping from the other room. *It's now or never.*

Sliding out from under the bed, he pulled himself to his feet. His knees felt wobbly. For one terrifying second, he thought his legs would not obey. They felt anchored to the floor. *Please don't let the shower stop,* he prayed. The shackles on his feet slowly lifted. He reached the door and turned the knob. It wouldn't open. He gaped at it, dumbfounded. *The latch.* He flipped the latch and turned the knob. The door opened easily, flooding the room with a gust of cool air. Without warning, the shower stopped. Chris stepped out before remembering: *The latch.* Quickly reopening the door, he flipped the lock, then closed it behind him as quietly as possible. Trembling with fear and relief, he tiptoed away from room 106, half expecting the door to fly open and a hairy hand to grab him at any moment. Making his retreat, his Nikes kicked up puffs of dust as he looked back only once.

By the time he reached his own room he was feeling a whole lot better. His legs were no longer shaking, and the feeling that he might have an "accident" if he didn't find a bathroom had vanished. The breeze cooled his skin and soothed his overloaded senses. *What now?* For a moment, Chris considered going to the police. But what real evidence did he have? *What else is going on?*

Anna's dog greeted Chris at the door of his room.

"What are you doing here, fella? Where's your owner?"

Bill stood looking into Chris's face, wagging his tail. He was panting hard. Knowing Anna must be close by, Chris trotted over to the motel lobby, wondering why she had come back. Thinking of her made him feel guilty. He had falsely accused her; he had been cutting and mean. *Some friend I've been.* Anna was not in the lobby. He ran over to the restaurant with Bill tagging at his heels. No Anna.

"Where is she, boy?"

Bill whined and groveled at his feet. His tongue dropped gobs of saliva onto the sidewalk. It was strange that Bill would be here without Anna, Chris thought. The dog seldom left her side, if he could help it. *Is Anna in trouble?* His mind began to go back over the events of the last thirty minutes, vexed by them. *"Leave the unexpected cargo to me—I'll take care of it. Accidents happen, right?"*

What was Mr. Reeves talking about? Where's Anna?

Chris could hardly bring himself to think that Anna might be in trouble. She was probably home, safe. *But what if she isn't? What if she's lying in the canyon somewhere, hurt. Accidents happen, right?*

"Bill! Come here, boy. Where's Anna?"

Again Bill whined, looking up into his face.

"Is she in trouble? Can you take me to her, fella?"

Chris didn't know if the dog understood him or not; but Bill barked and started running toward the trail leading to the canyon. He stopped and barked again, wagging his tail rapidly.

"All right, Bill. Let's go see if we can find her. I'll get Erick's horse. Stop barking, will ya?"

Coyote Canyon, 8:40 P.M.

Chris wasn't too surprised that Bill led him into Coyote Canyon. If there was such a thing as fate, he was sure it was calling to him now. Somehow he knew that the canyon held dark secrets—premonitions told him so. In a couple of days, when he would awake in a hospital bed, Chris would know just how true his premonitions could be.

The stillness in the canyon was a deception: static energy, elusive now, but the threat was real. The sky confirmed it. Thunderheads had already smothered any remaining fragments of daylight, reducing the world to a swarthy gray. Chris was thankful he'd brought a flashlight.

They were nearing the end of the box canyon where the old cliff dwellings were located. Bill was up ahead, barking hysterically and clawing at the sheer rock below the ruins. Chris reined in Erick's horse and dismounted. He pushed his fingers through his hair and looked up at the fortress-like walls. He could actually *feel* the silence.

What are we doing here, Bill?

There wasn't a sign of Anna. A solitary crow stared down at them from a rocky pinnacle. Chris looked around. He had never before experienced such silence. It was oppressive, suffocating.

"CAAAWK!"

The sound made the hair bristle on his neck.

Jeez! What am I doing here? The dog must be nuts! I must be nuts!

"ANNA!" he called out, the sound dying as soon as it left his lips. *No echo.*

Bill continued barking, stopping only long enough to intermittently paw at the rocky wall. The dog glared up at the cliff dwellings, then at the crow, worrying himself into circles. Chris wondered if it were possible for a dog to have a nervous breakdown.

"What is it, boy?"

She isn't up there. I know she isn't.

He was sure of it. No. He wasn't sure. Matter-of-fact, something told him she *was* up there. Something that started out as a small voice was now shouting inside his brain. *She's up there, buck-o. You're going*

to have to go up there and get her. She might be alive or she might not, but you're going to have to find out!

He swore to himself, stuffed the flashlight into his pants, and tied the reins of his horse to a piñon branch. He thought of Anna and how she had talked him out of foolishly trying to climb up to the ruins when they were here before. There was no one smart enough to talk him out of it this time.

"Anna, if you're up there, you *have* to be all right. Please . . ." he said aloud.

The finger- and toeholds leading up to the ruins were worn smooth. Chris was amazed that they were so shallow. It took all his strength just to pull himself up to the lowest set of niches. He paused, trying to figure out his next move. If he started out with the wrong foot, it might be impossible to correct later, which could be disastrous. Stretched out like a spider on the sheer rock, he dug his foot into the next smooth cavity; at the same time, he clawed at the grainy stone above him, searching for a secure hold.

Sweat stung his eyes as he clung to the coarse face of the cliff, grappling for each small indentation. He didn't dare look down for fear of leaning out too far—the weight of his body in that position would surely cause him to fall. His feet groped for toeholds that his fingers had grasped earlier. He couldn't help but think of what a struggle it was going to be to climb back down. *If* he was lucky enough to make it up.

The muscles in his legs quivered spasmodically. His chest heaved, and his lips tingled; he felt dizzy. With a final burst of energy, Chris boosted himself up to the ledge, digging in with his elbows. Swinging his right foot up, he used both elbows to pull the lower half of his body up atop the ledge. There he rested, staring at the dark shadow of rock above him, blowing air like an unhinged bellow.

Chris wasn't sure how long he lay there, but finally his heart calmed and his chest slowed to a sane rhythm. It was now totally dark. Bill had stopped barking. *It's so quiet in here,* he thought. The calm was somehow ominous.

Pulling out his flashlight, he clicked it on and ventured over to the ruins. They were larger than they had looked from below. His light shot across the rubble of multi-roomed structures, causing shadows to flee to the deepest corners of the decaying, old buildings. The beam roamed over the broken walls, the piles of rocks and mortar. Peering into a T-shaped doorway, he cast the light inside. The room was small and had a fusty, charcoal-like smell. The sunken dirt floor was littered with sandstone bricks and potshards. *No Anna.*

Bill started barking again, sounding far away. Chris passed cautiously from building to building, throwing light onto the tumbledown walls and crumbling towers, exploring the hidden recesses of each dwelling.

Coming to a large open area, Chris danced his light over the debris. At the far end stood a wall; a stepped entryway led to another level of buildings. What at first appeared to be rocks were scattered about everywhere; large mounds of dirt lay piled up on the ground. His next discovery left him gaping in shock, his flashlight skimming over the gruesome scene.

It looked like something out of a grade-B horror movie. Bones littered the area. Although he was no archaeologist, he knew human bones when he saw them. The beam from his flashlight rested on what looked like a rib cage, until the light started shaking too badly. Obviously, he was standing in a graveyard, a plundered graveyard. Stepping lightly around the cratered areas, Chris noticed that a lot of the holes had something in them. He shined his light closer. The beam bounced back, reflecting off some kind of glossy material. *Plastic bags!* Black, wastebasket-size bags were lying in there, stuffed with something. He didn't want to look. He had to. Pulling a bag out of a hole, Chris shoved the flashlight into the opening and braved a peek inside.

He had expected to find something far worse than what he encountered: broken pots! Large pieces of pottery, their bold, geometric patterns mixed together in a collage of broken shapes, lay jumbled together.

It dawned on him then. *Hadn't Mr. Reeves said something about "waking the dead"? Is this what he meant? But where's Anna?*

"Anna, are you up here?" he shouted.

Silence.

Following the flashlight beam, Chris worked his way over to the wall. Suddenly, a heavy beating of wings exploded above his head. *Bats?*

"Phew! It's only a crow," he said aloud.

The large bird alighted on the rocks not far from where he stood. Without fear, it hopped toward him. Chris didn't like it. The crow was *too* bold.

He tried shooing it away with a swipe of his flashlight, the beam throwing shadows into a hodgepodge of tangled phantoms. The crow flurried its wings, glared at him, and refused to retreat an inch. Chris reached down for a piece of loose stone. "Get!" he said, throwing the rock awkwardly. He missed. The bird hissed and flurried its wings again. Feeling shaken, Chris reached for another rock. The eerie creature threw out its wings and beat the air vehemently. In a blink it was gone, disappearing into the darkness from where it had come.

Chris would have turned and run, but his knees were too weak. He was scared, scared like he'd never been before. *No Anna anywhere, I've got to get out of here.*

Just then he heard something, a faint knocking from somewhere. The knocking was followed by a muffled sound. Instinctively, he drew away from the noise, pinpointing it as coming from the far end of the hollow. He was sure that whatever it was, it had to be inside the small building above the wall.

Chris had never considered himself brave. If it weren't for the fact that his friend was missing and quite probably in danger, he never would have come here. He never would have climbed up the crumbling old steps at the wall. He never would have approached the dwelling with the strange sounds. He never would have dared step through the low, T-shaped entrance, and he would never have stumbled onto the most important find in his life.

Shining the light into the darkness, he faltered when it settled on a small, moving bundle. To his utter amazement, the light illuminated a girl lying on the dirt floor, tied, gagged, and huddled in the corner. Her long hair hung in thick tangles about her face. The blaring white shock of the flashlight attacked her frightened, darting eyes. The eyes of Anna Joe.

He ran over to her, fumbling with the light while trying to untie the knots around her wrists.

"Mmmffhhh!"

"Right. The gag."

Holding the flashlight with his knees, he went to work. Chris winced as he pulled on the scarf. It was tied tightly enough to be cutting into her mouth. Finally, his excited fingers were able to get one knot undone. Soon the scarf loosened and dropped from her face.

Anna sighed. "Thank God."

"Here, let me get these," Chris said, digging his fingers into the rope around her wrists. "Jeez, they're so tight!"

After tearing a fingernail or two, he started seeing progress. At length, the ties loosened enough for Anna to slip her hands free. Chris noticed the red lines of broken skin. The rope around her ankles was another matter. It had to be twenty feet or longer, wrapped and tied after each circuit around her legs, and finally secured to a beam by the wall.

"I'm afraid this is going to take awhile. What happened? Who did this to you?" Chris had the sick feeling he already knew.

Anna seemed not to hear him. She stared down at her wrists, looking confused.

"Are you hurt?" he asked.

She shook her head, brushing hair away from her face absently. "I'm okay. Just so thirsty."

"Oh great," he said, "I didn't even bring a canteen. Anna, you look awful."

She forced a smile. "Thanks. You always say such nice things."

One knot loosened and then dissolved. Chris unwrapped a layer and began working on another. "We'll be out of here in no time," he ventured, trying to sound confident. He looked into her eyes. "I wish I had some water for you."

"That's okay. I'm just glad you found me. The more I think about it, the more I'm sure they planned on getting rid of me for good."

"Who?"

"Reeves, of course. He was with some other jerks. They grabbed me after my horse sprained her leg." Anna then explained why she had come into the canyon and how the kidnapping had happened.

"But why did they nab you?" he asked.

"I don't know. Maybe they thought I saw too much. It sounded like they had some big deal going on tonight. They must've thought I'd squeal on 'em. They're pothunters, you know."

"I know. They've dug up this place like mad. I heard Mr. Reeves say something about 'waking the dead.' I guess this is what he meant."

Gaining on another knot, Chris quickly told her about his past five hours. He finished with his account of Bill leading him here. "And here we are, with nothing to worry about but Mr. Reeves and a gang of pothunters, kidnappers, and likely murderers on their way back at any minute."

"I'll take care of that creep," Anna vowed, touching the tender corners of her mouth. Without saying anything, Chris doubted if she could.

"Well, I don't think we need to worry about getting even, not right now anyway. Besides, 'what goes around comes around,' " Chris said, dredging up one of his dad's favorite old sayings. Maybe it didn't quite fit the situation, but it sounded good.

Anna threw him one of her infamous looks of contempt. "You're so wise," she cooed.

Chris felt a slow, unwilling grin stretching his mouth. " 'He who laughs last, his laugh lasts,' " he quoted. "Or something like that."

They looked at each other and started giggling. Soon they were laughing. Laughing so hard that their eyes watered. It felt good—life felt real good right now.

"You know," Chris said, changing the mood and looking serious again. "I really owe you an apology. I was a real jerk back at the motel. You were right about Reeves all along. I was really gullible. I wouldn't blame you if you hated my guts."

He was rewarded with one of the warmest and most tender smiles Anna had ever offered. In that instant, Chris thought she looked beautiful.

"In the Navajo language there isn't a word for 'I'm sorry.' If a person is sorry, he just doesn't do it again." She shrugged. "It's that easy."

She was watching Chris pull the rope through a loose knot; fine hairs of hemp sprinkled onto her jeans.

"Is that the last one?"

"Yeah. Got it. Come on."

Chris helped Anna to her feet and walked her to the low entrance. She was shaky at first, but her legs strengthened with each step. As soon as he felt she was able to walk on her own, he darted back inside and came back with the pile of rope.

"We'll need this to get down," he explained.

Chris knew they had to get away from the ruins as fast as possible. Neither of them needed to be reminded of the danger. It was best not to think of what would happen if they were caught. Passing the holes and piles of bones, neither spoke.

The air greeting them at the front of the ruins felt fresh and invigorating. Chris quickly tied the ropes together and fastened one end to a fallen ceiling beam; he threw the other end over the side of the ledge, where it disappeared into the darkness. Bill started barking again, sounding like he was going loco. Chris made a mock salute and then began climbing down the rope.

"Be careful," Anna said, watching him slide over the side of the cliff.

The rope made the descent much easier than the climb up, and within minutes Chris reached the end of the rope. It wasn't quite long enough, so the last six feet were a free fall. He landed easily and then called up to Anna.

Tossing the flashlight to him, she followed. Crumbling sandstone rained down behind her as she skidded over the side, working her way to the jump-off point. Bill was delirious with joy, pouncing on her as soon as she dropped.

"Stop it, Bill!" she cried, laughing and trying to push him away. "Yuck! You're slobbering all over me!" Bill was undaunted. His tail sped up to maximum level as he jumped up and down and in circles, the sole member of the welcoming committee. "You brought Chris here, huh boy? Such a good dog. You saved my life!"

Chris watched, smiling. It was good to be out in the open again. A flash of lightning glowed behind the upper rim of the canyon. Looking up, he saw thick clouds backlit by the moon, their edges tainted in silver. Another glimpse of lightning, this time followed by thunder.

Finding Erick's horse, he called over to Anna. "Come on, let's get out of here. We'll ride double."

"Where's Pepper?" Anna queried. "I've got food and water in her saddlebags. I'm so thirsty."

Chris flashed his light around. "I don't know. I never saw her. Maybe Reeves took her so there'd be no trace of where you were. Come on, Anna, we've got to get out of here!"

Anna opened her mouth to protest, but Chris hushed her. "Listen . . ."

"What?"

"Can't you hear that?"

Tilting her head to one side, she listened. She heard it now. A pounding sound—not unlike the sound they had heard the first night they were in Coyote Canyon. It grew louder. The tempo quickened, the sound beating the sky somewhere above. It was getting closer. Like magic, the blackness above suddenly ripped open. Lights shot out of the sky and headed toward them.

〰〰 *10* 〰〰

SECRET PASSAGE

Coyote Canyon, 9:45 P.M.

"TURN OFF THE LIGHT!" Anna shouted.

Chris snapped off the flashlight and stared up at the approaching lights. The chopping grew louder, pounding the air and echoing off the cliff walls. Realization cut through the clouds with it—*a helicopter.* It was closing in on them.

"Oh no," Chris muttered. "Anna, we've got to run—*it's them!*"

"Not out there! They'll see us."

Grabbing his arm, she pulled him back toward the walls of the canyon. Half running, half stumbling, they turned and fled into the sanctuary of fallen boulders, into the safety of the night shadows. They peered out at the sight, awestruck. It was scary, hypnotic. An image flashed through Chris's mind of a frightened mouse staring at the deadly eyes of a snake, paralyzed. *The hunted and the hunter.*

He glanced at Anna. She appeared disheveled, yet cool, concentrating. Bill was next to her, looking scared. She stroked the dog's neck, reassuring him.

We're going to beat them, he promised himself.

The helicopter hovered at tree level, not over a hundred yards from where they were hiding. Its lights scanned the rocks, like blinding white eyes, searching. Finally, it lurched, descended further, and then abruptly landed on the canyon floor. The disturbance was too much for Erick's horse; the mare yanked her reins loose and bolted as the whirling blades threw sand and tumbleweeds into the enraged air. As the engine shut down, the pounding slowed and the noise gradually abated. The clapping stopped. A soft humming sound drifted from the cockpit. The blinding spotlights blinked off, leaving only a dim, blue light burning from inside. It grew quiet.

Small, white lights appeared outside the helicopter. Voices followed. The lights bobbed up and down, separated, and then drew closer. Suddenly, a familiar voice rang out: "Get the ladders . . . let's move quickly, guys."

Mr. Reeves.

Chris felt goose bumps between his shoulderblades.

Metal clanged. Heavy footsteps trudged back and forth from the helicopter to the cliff. More voices. Laughter. Lights and silhouetted figures moved to and fro. Lights climbed up to the ruins. Shuffling noises. Silence. A shout.

"Hey, Bob! The kid . . . she's gone!"

Too near for comfort, Chris and Anna heard Reeves moan. He swore, moving closer. Rays from his flashlight skipped over the rocks. Chris's heart fluttered in his chest like a bird chained to a perch.

"How in the . . . ? I don't believe it! One stupid kid messing up the whole operation! Tom, Hal, grab what we've already bagged. Forget the rest. We'll have to get out of here. Quick. Arnie, grab a rifle and comb the area—she might not be far off."

A tiny light flicked on, illuminating Reeves's face. His eyes looked like narrow slits as he held the lighter flame up to his cigarette. His whole countenance looked different. He seemed thinner, harder, reptilian. His lighter had to chase the tip of his cigarette for a few seconds, betraying the fact that he was more than a little shaky. The acrid smell of tobacco smoke reached Chris's nostrils.

After what seemed like ages, he walked back toward the helicopter. Another man strolled over to him.

"I ain't gonna shoot no kid," the big man said.

"You will if I say so," Reeves countered. "Look. If she gets away, we'll be facing a kidnapping rap on top of everything else. Do you want that? It's going too good, Arnie. We'll be able to retire after this haul."

"I don't like it," Arnie complained.

"Hey, I don't like it any more than you, but find her and do what you have to do."

Arnie lumbered over to the helicopter. He came out carrying a rifle, thumbed something into his pocket, and walked off into the night. The beam from his flashlight darted across the landscape, growing smaller. For a moment Mr. Reeves watched him. Finally, he shook his head, flicked his cigarette into the grass, and climbed up the ladder to the ruins.

Chris turned to Anna. "Let's get out of here," he whispered, gently touching her shoulder.

Anna shook her head. "We can't. They'll find us." She was trembling. "They really want to kill me!"

"We're not going to get caught. We're going to get out of here," Chris reassured her, like it was already settled. "Come on."

With Bill leading, Anna and Chris quietly circled the canyon, hugging the rocks and bushes closest to the cliff. The ruins were across from them now; the pothunters' flashlights looked like fireflies flitting in the dark. Anna felt better now that they were moving. To Chris, the whole crazy thing seemed like a dream. *This sort of stuff doesn't happen in real life, only on TV.* Getting careless, he slipped on some loose rock, causing a small avalanche to skip and clatter into the unknown. Afraid that it might've been heard across the arroyo, they ducked into a low-ceilinged hollow, half hidden in cheat grass. From their hiding place, they surveyed the area. It appeared safe.

Chris wondered where the big ape with the gun was. *Is he sitting out there somewhere in the dark, watching?* Above the canyon rim, a black thunderhead lit itself with internal lightning, flashed once more, and then faded back into black.

Bill sniffed around, inspecting their little hollow. He disappeared behind them.

"Well, what do you think?" Anna asked.

"I think we're just about clear. When we get around them, we'll be safe," he said. This was only partly true, of course, and Anna would know it.

She said nothing but privately doubted if their troubles were anywhere near being over. As if to confirm her suspicions, Bill started barking.

"Shhh!" she hissed. "Come here, Bill. Where are you?"

The barking came from their hiding place, but somehow it sounded far away. Chris stared into the darkness behind him: *apparently, the hollow goes back a heck of a lot further.* He flicked his flashlight on and off quickly, trying to get a glimpse of the back wall.

Darkness.

Not knowing if he was doing it for Anna's sake or his own, Chris reached out for her hand. Cautiously, he took a step. Then another. Again, he flicked on the flashlight; the beam was instantly swallowed by the blackness. He pointed it upward before snapping it off. The ceiling was low enough to touch but high enough that they could walk upright without worrying about bumping into it.

"It's a cave!" Chris exclaimed.

The Passage, 10:10 P.M.

Cool and damp, the tunnel seemed to take them in and then tighten around them. Chris looked back over his shoulder. The entrance was no longer visible, obscured by the curve of the wall. He bumped into rock and felt grainy powder crumble onto his hand.

"Turn on your light," Anna said. "No one's going to see it now."

The beam sliced through the blackness in front of them, but it didn't dispel it. To their growing wonder, they were penetrating deeper and deeper into the rock. The passage was wide enough to walk in with outstretched hands and still not be able to touch both sides. The floor

felt wet beneath their sneakers, lush with some kind of algae.

Something on the wall caught Chris's eye. He pointed the beam on it. Behind him, Anna gasped. She pushed him closer, eager to study the picture carved in the rock.

"The humpbacked flute player!" Anna cried. "It's just like the one we found in the skull."

Chris nodded. She was right. Scores of petroglyphs were etched into the sandstone. One image, the largest, was a figure of the horned stick man, hunched over and playing a flute; his gross-looking hump stuck out from his back as he played his silent music. It was an exact replica of the figure on their amulet. Chris recalled that evening of discovery in his room; it seemed like such a long time ago. That was back when it was all a game, a harmless mystery.

"Any connection to the amulet we've got?" Chris asked.

Anna looked pensive. "Might be. Maybe it's all part of the same code, or message. Maybe we were supposed to find this place."

This thought led to a sudden, paralyzing fear, something far scarier than Reeves and his goons. For a moment Chris felt the way you do when you suddenly realize you want off the roller coaster before it reaches the top and begins its downward plunge. You know it's too late, but you can't help but wish you had never climbed aboard. There was nothing to do now but hold on tight. He had an intuitive flash: *We're being carried here. There's no getting off. There's no change in direction. Something is pulling us forward.*

"Chris, do you think we should keep going? We can always turn around," Anna said, seeming to read his mind.

His intuition dissolved into a meaningless jumble of thoughts and then disappeared as suddenly as it had surfaced.

"No. We'll keep going. Wherever it leads, we're bound to be safer and better hidden. Here—take my hand again. We don't know if there are other connecting caves or not. We can't afford to lose each other."

They crept onward, finding confidence in the small ray of light Chris held in front of them. The beam cast strange shapes all around. Menacing black-cloaked figures appeared to be springing up from the ground in front of them, though none reached out to seize them. The light flashed through the shadowy figures as through columns of smoke, shrinking them before they rose again in the darkness and empty silence to become giants.

Chris and Anna kept moving. Ahead of them, Chris thought he heard an intake of breath.

He froze.

"Did you hear that?"

"What?" Anna asked, sounding frightened.

"Never mind. It was nothing. I guess I'm just hearing things," he said, but didn't really believe it. He *had* heard something. *Maybe it's Bill*, he thought, again knowing it wasn't. He felt gooseflesh on his arms. A sense of oppressiveness was growing in him, a feeling that the cave was dangerous and alive, a feeling that there were things in it aware of their passing.

Anna shuddered.

"What is it?" he asked.

"I thought I heard something whispering."

Chris swallowed hard. She said she heard *something* whispering— not *someone*.

"Phew!" he gasped. "I don't like this, not any of it."

Suddenly, Chris felt something touch his leg. He almost jumped out of his skin. He screamed. Anna screamed. He flashed the light down, gritting his teeth, dreading what he might see.

It was only Bill.

"Oh jeez, I don't believe it," he said, feeling both relieved and foolish. Anna started giggling. It was contagious. Soon they were both laughing, shaking uncontrollably.

Still feeling embarrassed, Chris moved on with Anna following at his heels. His heart thudded in his temples as he led them through the tunnel. All sense of time melted into the darkness.

"I think we're coming to an opening!" Chris finally announced, feeling fresh air touching his face. "Can you feel it?"

Anna nodded. "Hurry!" she panted.

To their relief, the tunnel opened up to the outside world. Chris felt something in his chest loosen a little. Neither of them could guess what lay ahead.

Home of the flute player, 10:30 P.M.

"Wow!"

"What a cool place!" Anna exclaimed, looking around at the rocks that surrounded the dark patch of meadow in front of them. Thunder softly rumbled overhead, sounding ominous.

"Yeah, cool all right," he said. "I think we've found our flute player's home."

Anna looked at her watch. "Shine the light over here, Chris. Can you believe it? It's only 10:30! I thought it had to be almost morning."

He nodded solemnly. "I wish it were," he said, moving the light around the strange place they'd found. *Unbelievable all right.*

Dear Mom: Went camping after all . . . Having a great time. Oh yeah, almost forgot to mention—the day picked up a little. There's a real nice man named Mr. Reeves, who asked another nice man to find my friend and shoot her. Yeah, the girl I hang out with, the one I thought stole my skeleton head. It turns out she never had it—the kidnappers had it all along. The kidnappers? Didn't I mention them? Yeah, the grave robbers. They're one and the same. Boy oh boy, I'll write more later—if I live to tell about it. P. S. Say "hi" to Dad for me when he drops by with the alimony payment (he hasn't had time to write me yet). I hope he's kept up on the ol' Family Life Insurance Policy. You never know when something like that might come in handy. Well, better run (get it?). Love, Chris.

It was quiet, with just a few insects making their nocturnal sounds. The tunnel had opened up to a small, grassy meadow, surrounded on all sides by curious-looking rock formations, the kind that seem to take on familiar shapes when you use your imagination. Wildflowers covered the ground; the vegetation parted in the middle for a stream which trickled off to some unknown place. The small brook was fed by a spring that formed a tiny pool and cascaded over a low tumble of rocks. Anasazi ruins loomed on the ledge above them.

Bill barked and tilted his head to one side, trying to make some sense of everything. Amazingly, they weren't alone. A scattering of sheep and cows were grazing in the center of the meadow. The animals had somehow found their way into the unspoiled pasture. *This explains the mysterious disappearance of cattle and sheep in Coyote Canyon,* Chris thought.

"Look, it's Pepper!" Anna cried.

Sure enough, the spotted mare was grazing close by. Evidently, she had ventured into the meadow earlier and was now one more statistic of missing animals in Coyote Canyon. Pepper stomped and whinnied.

Anna slowly approached her until she was close enough to reach for the fallen reins. The horse never even bothered to raise her head—she was too busy taking advantage of the choice feeding.

"Stay here, Bill," Chris commanded, grabbing the dog's fur. "We don't need you running over there and spooking her."

Bill cooperated. He sat watching Anna and her horse, panting good-humoredly.

"I've got her!" Anna shouted. "Good girl. Let's take a look at those saddlebags, okay?"

Anna returned with the leather bags and dropped them at Chris's feet. "You'd better turn off your light, it's getting weaker," she said. "Come on, have a seat and let me show you what I've got for us."

Chris sat down in the grass beside her, watching as she rummaged through the bags. Finding her canteen, she drank greedily and then passed it over to him. Next were the sandwiches. They were devoured in minutes; peanut butter and jelly had never tasted better.

Anna sifted through her things until she found a thin wool blanket, which she threw over her shoulders. She offered to share half with Chris, but he shook his head and said he'd pass. Its warmth would've been great, but being that close to Anna would've been a bit uncomfortable. After all, he was only twelve.

An hour later they were still sitting there, feeling content.

"Heck of a day," Anna said. Even in the gloom Chris could see the dark half circles under her eyes.

"I must look awful."

"No. You look fine—nice. Really."

Actually, he thought she still looked pretty, maybe even prettier than usual, although he never in a million years would have dared say such a thing to her.

Anna peered at him, amused. "You're such a gentleman," she crooned, pretending to primp her hair. "I just LUHHV when you talk like that!"

Chris was momentarily flustered, feeling a blush rising to his cheeks. He had said it in a natural way, but now he felt a little weird about it. He dropped his eyes, retreating from Anna's smile.

"I'm just teasing you," she said, her eyes dancing.

Chris smiled shyly, and they both fell silent, but it wasn't an awkward silence.

Anna put her arms on her knees, her head in her arms, and yawned. It was going to be a long night. Chris found himself glancing sideways at her from time to time. He couldn't help but observe the way she absently pushed her hair back, the way she tossed her head. He looked at her small, delicate mouth, the long, graceful nose. All of these things delighted him. He could not have said why, but they did. It was time to get moving, time to find a way out of this mess, but he would sit for just a minute longer, because it was good to look at her, to be with her.

A jagged bolt of lightning struck nearby; thunder followed. Somewhere in the darkness a crow cawed.

~~~~ *11* ~~~~

THE DARK NIGHT

Home of the flute player, midnight

FEARFUL OF BEING CAUGHT in the oncoming storm, Chris and Anna climbed the talus slope leading up to the old ruins. Only a few walls remained, but the dwellings were deep enough in the hollow to provide an adequate roof over their heads. Chris gathered dead piñon branches for kindling while Anna searched her saddlebags for matches. They were soon huddled over a tiny fire, absorbing its warmth, watching the sparks drifting up into the darkness. Bill kept himself busy nosing around through the other chambers.

A flash of blue-white lightning illuminated Anna's face; its booming thunder drowned out what she was saying.

"Huh?"

"The skull," she repeated. "That's why he wanted the skull. He knew it was important. Of course, he knew we'd suspect him of stealing it since we only showed it to Erick and him. That's why he made up that stuff about seeing me coming out of your room. Reeves must've known you were gone that night. He put the blame on me so he wouldn't be suspected. Pretty clever 'cause it worked."

Chris avoided her eyes for a second. It was hard to believe he could have ever doubted Anna.

"Well," he said, "I'm glad we found the amulet before the skull was stolen. I wonder if that's what he was after?"

Anna shrugged, poking a stick into the coals. "Maybe, and maybe not. Maybe he didn't really know what he'd find, but he figured the skull would somehow tell him something."

"Sure," Chris interjected. "Like the whereabouts of this place—a pothunter's dream."

"How would the skull tell him that?" she asked.

Chris grew excited as a number of answers unraveled in his brain. "Easy," he said. "Remember where we found the skull?"

"Yeah. It was on the ledge."

"Right! It was setting straight across the canyon from the cave. It was pointing, actually staring right at the cave's entrance. Whoever put the skull there wanted to leave it as a marker so others could find this place. But who'd go to the trouble of making all those clues?"

"That's simple," Anna quipped. "*Who* would've had a knife that's a hundred years old? It could've been a soldier, or it could've been someone who took it from a soldier. And *who* would've wanted to leave clues leading to a secret hiding place—a place almost completely unknown since the Anasazi lived here? *Who* would've needed a place to hide?"

Chris shook his head, perplexed.

Anna continued: "Remember my grandfather telling us there were old stories about a secret hiding place? Suppose a few Navajo knew about this hideout when Kit Carson's soldiers were rounding up everybody. Suppose they wanted others to be able to find it."

Chris's eyes widened with comprehension. "Brilliant, my dear Watson! That's got to be right. Somebody came up with the keen idea of writing down a sort of code on the rock, right next to the old Anasazi pictures. Who'd know the difference? Not the soldiers. But Indians looking for a hideout would. They'd understand the picture, find the tree with the knife in it, and that would lead them to the skull."

"And the skull would lead them to this place," Anna added. "The perfect hideout."

"Uh-huh. There's plenty of room, there's water, and I'll bet they stashed food up here somewhere. A person could hide in a place like this for a long time. But why the amulet?"

Anna raised her eyebrows, just as a spear of lightning sizzled in the sky.

"Why stick an Anasazi amulet inside the skull?" he queried.

"I wonder," Anna mused, "if it was a sign to let people know it was an Anasazi place. Remember, a lot of Navajo today are still afraid to enter Anasazi ruins. They're afraid of the *chindi*. Maybe it was a kind of warning to tell them they would be entering at their own risk. It would also give them a chance to decide against going in."

Chris shrugged. "Makes sense to me. Anyway, it's a good thing Reeves never found this place—it would be all dug up by now."

There was another flash of lightning, an explosion of thunder, and then the rain came. It started soft enough, but within minutes it was hurtling out of the sky in torrents. Its fierceness was alarming. Chris and Anna watched in silence, unable to speak above the loud clamor of water slapping rock.

With the cloudburst came new fragrances. Rocks and trees gave off fresh scents, sweet and clean. The squall let up a little, tempering to a steady downpour. Chris wasn't aware of how long he watched the rain, but when he looked back at Anna, she was sleeping.

She lay huddled in a ball, her hands tucked between her knees and her head resting on the saddlebags. Bill was faithfully curled up at her feet. Chris walked over and covered her shoulders with the blanket. She stirred a little. Looking down at her, he thought she looked beautiful. It seemed to Chris that their relationship had somehow changed in these past few hours. He was suddenly aware of how he looked at her differently, thought of her differently. It was a little confusing.

Throwing another log on the fire, he sat staring into the flames.

The glowing coals twinkled. He began to feel drowsy. The patter of rain had a tranquilizing effect, soothing, comforting, lulling him to sleep.

In limbo between consciousness and sleep, his eyes started playing tricks on him. Rock formations, illuminated by the firelight, began melting and twisting into human-like shapes. Faces. Tortured-looking faces.

Chris jerked himself awake. He immediately looked over at Anna, relieved to see her still asleep. *Just a dream.*

The fire had died to a few glowing embers. Yet, somehow everything seemed brighter, like the rocks were giving off an inner radiance. *The rocks.*

He sat up and poked a stick into the smoldering coals, causing a rebirth of flames. *That's ridiculous,* he thought. But just the same, he looked around, having the uneasy feeling of being watched.

Chris pulled his eyes away from the rocks. *No way,* he told himself, trying to think of something else. It was no use; he looked again. The rocks stared back at him, the way the eyes in some pictures seemed to always be looking at you no matter where you were in the room. It was funny how he hadn't noticed until now how life-like the formations seemed. The shapes and textures in the stones could have been chiseled by a sculptor carving out the hidden image within. The shapes looked alive, constantly unfolding, changing. He thought he saw faces; he stared at them, fascinated at first and then horrified. His heart began to speed up. His breathing came faster. Not possible. He had *not* seen faces in the rock. There were no ghosts, or *chindi,* or whatever they were called. He closed his eyes for a moment.

He looked again. To his growing horror, Chris saw that the rocks *really were looking at him.* The faces twisted and bulged, leering, grimacing, shrieking in silence. He looked away. His senses felt overloaded.

A great black crow flapped out of the shadows with a raucous caw, an explosion of flapping. It alighted on the wall nearby. The creature hissed at him, its eyes glimmering.

"Go on! Get!" Chris snapped, throwing his stick at the evil-looking creature.

The bird stared at him, defiant and unafraid. Finally, it flew off into the darkness, leaving Chris trembling.

"Anna!" he cried. "Anna, wake up!"

Anna sat up, blinking and looking confused. "What is it?"

"Tell me I'm seeing things, please. Oh jeez, look over there!"

Bewildered, Anna followed his gaze. She stared at the rocks for a long minute, mesmerized, disbelieving, and finally shocked. Her hands flew to her cheeks. Her eyes widened.

The faces in the rock billowed and writhed.

"*Chindi!*" she screamed.

"This," he said, "is crazy."

Jumping to his feet, he grabbed Anna's hand, seized the flashlight, and dashed madly down the treacherous path.

Footsteps echoed in their ears as they fled into the night. The steadily weakening flashlight bobbed wildly, throwing shadows along the cliff walls. Shadows leaped out of nowhere, chasing along at their sides, then flying ahead, then falling back once more, nipping at their heels.

They made it to the tunnel's entrance. Suddenly, a blinding flash of blue-white light illuminated the face of Mr. Reeves.

"Anna!" Chris screamed.

Too late. Reeves grabbed Anna's arm, yanking her hard enough that she lost her grip on Chris's hand. She fell to her knees. Chris ran, stumbling, looking back over his shoulder. Another man's face appeared—Arnie. He stared at Chris, his small eyes looking pig-like in his broad face. His massive bulk hovered over Anna.

"Let her go!" Chris screamed hoarsely.

Growling, Bill suddenly appeared out of nowhere and leapt at the giant. As graceful as a ballet dancer, Arnie side-stepped the dog and swung his rifle like a baseball bat. Chris heard a sickening thud, a yelp, and then silence.

Without a second thought, Chris picked up a rock and threw it. Under the circumstances, the projectile should have never found its target. But it did. The chunk of sandstone hit Arnie squarely above the eyebrow. He hollered, holding a huge hand to his forehead. In that instant, Anna kicked Reeves in the shin, causing him to lose his hold of her. She made a dash for it.

The image of what happened next was permanently burned into Chris's memory: Anna ran. He ran. Shouts. A gun shot. He looked back—in time to see Arnie still holding the rifle in aiming position. Anna was falling.

"No!" he cried.

In that instant, Chris felt a tremor. Reeves and Arnie felt it, too. They looked around, dumbfounded. Arnie screamed, pointing at the rocks.

If Chris still had any doubts of what he'd seen earlier, they vanished. In fact, he would never doubt what he witnessed at that moment for the rest of his life.

Chris felt thousands of tiny brushes against his skin as he stepped forward, as though he'd walked into a dense cloud of invisible gnats. The sensation made his skin crawl. He turned around to face the cliff wall. All the breath left his body at once.

The rocks surrounding them began to tremble. Large masses started to warp, twisting and melting into grotesque body shapes—a hand here, a foot there, more faces, mouths with animal teeth. Faces grew beaks; eyes became round and carnivorous, changing into bird-like monsters, then evolving again into human forms. The metamorphosis was horrifying; it was like looking at everything through a carnival mirror, where images bent into contorted, absurd distortions. Even the air changed, becoming liquid-like, thick, foul smelling, the breath of something dead—long dead.

Chris heard one of the men scream again, but it sounded muffled and far away. Suddenly, the rock faces began to buckle, caving in on all sides. Stone walls cracked, rumbling deep within. Flakes of sandstone, then chips, then boulders, rained over their heads.

Covering his head with his hands, Chris dropped to his knees. It seemed like the whole place was caving in on him. He caught a last glimpse of Reeves and Arnie disappearing back into the tunnel, fleeing

for their lives.

At some point the quaking stopped. It grew still. In the stillness came the dark. Not the kind of darkness that comes with a moonless night, but the darkness of a grave, a void without life. And there were voices. Panting. Shuddering. Whispering.

Chris groped for his flashlight; finding it, he snapped it on. The waning light barely penetrated the opaque blackness. Voices continued, whispering with hysteric urgency. Demons in the dark.

He spotted Anna.

Under any other conditions, the voices would have surely driven him mad. Their cries filled his ears, his soul. They clamped around his heart with icy fingers. But his mind was unwavering. Anna needed him. After pushing his way through the gauntlet of murmuring voices, he knelt down beside her. He touched her shoulder gently. Finally, he turned her over.

She's dead. No. Don't even think it. She's going to be fine. Just knocked out, that's all.

He knew he had to get her out of here.

She's dead.

Getting to his feet, Chris frantically searched for Pepper. The horse, lame or not, could carry her. No sign of her anywhere. *All this craziness must've spooked her,* he thought. Chris walked a few feet further, hating to leave Anna for even a second. No horse to be found. He looked back at Anna, lying crumpled and still. *What does it matter. She's dead. No! Don't think it.*

Chris returned to his friend, feeling helpless. The voices continued, babbling at him in waves. He couldn't understand what they were saying, and he didn't want to. The darkness was so thick, so heavy.

She's dead.

She can't be.

She doesn't move.

So?

Chris felt dizzy. Seeing Anna lying there was too much; he was going to pass out.

I can't. She needs me.

Everything started to spin. He shook his head.

Voices.

He listened, thinking in a way that was not quite verbal that he was not in the real world, but in some terrible dream that was trying to claim him forever.

"Anna?"

She didn't answer.

"Please, Anna."

Touching her, Chris felt something in her hair. Blood. A trickle ran down the back of her head. He started crying. Taking ahold of one arm, he lifted it, then slipped two fingers under her wrist, feeling for a pulse. He couldn't find one.

Demon voices seemed to mock him.

Concentrate.

He found a pulse, a barely perceptible throb. She was still alive.

Alive!

With renewed hope, Chris examined her more closely. Her face felt cold. A fine mist of sweat lined her brow. He touched the back of her head; his fingers again felt the warm wetness of blood.

"Anna?"

Nothing.

He had to get her to some help fast. Since she couldn't walk, he would carry her. Still holding the flashlight, he gently picked her up. His muscles cried out at the strain. He pushed himself, making his muscles move and move.

Fear of losing Anna drove Chris back through the tunnel with greater determination than he would've had for his own survival. Going inside the cave was like entering the pit of hades. Whispering voices reached their zenith. The babbling rose to a horrifying level, sometimes melodious, other times ranting with insane discordance.

A lifetime later he reached the other end. The voices quieted.

Chris saw that there were no longer lights up in the ruins: the pothunters were gone. His horse was gone, too. He continued walking, carrying Anna in his arms as he would have carried a baby; her weight now seemed less than that of a small child.

For hours he trudged forward. His mind was no longer aware of pain, sore muscles, or time. Although his heart felt like bursting, his brain demanded that he push on. Anna needed help. Anna needed him.

From time to time he put her down long enough to regain feeling in his arms, lest he should drop her. As soon as he felt able, he continued carrying her. He fell to his knees once, got up, and fell again. He *willed* himself to continue, phasing in and out of sensibility, lumbering forward.

He felt feverish. Anna was motionless, no longer seeming as light as a child. His tortured muscles screamed for relief from their burden. Somewhere along the way Chris noticed he was still carrying the flashlight, the batteries long dead. He let it drop from his hand. The darkness was lifting, changing to a bluish gray.

More than once he realized he was in tears, staggering through the great lonely canyon. His hair was plastered to his forehead. Sweat dripped from his face, from under his arms, his back. He grew weaker, shakier. Shivers racked his body. He tried to turn his mind away from his own misery and to concentrate on helping Anna. She was so still—too still.

He set her down and examined her. There was no longer a pulse.

"Oh no," he cried aloud, feeling for a pulse again. "No, Anna. Please, no." He couldn't find a pulse.

She's dead.

Rocking her like a baby, Chris started sobbing. He told her she would be all right. He *insisted* that she would live. Half out of his mind with grief and despair, he continued rocking her. Blubbering, he wept until his eyes were nearly swollen shut. He picked her up and started walking again. In his mind he pictured her alive and smiling, pouting, teasing. Grief and exhaustion overtook him. He prayed, cursed, ranted and raved, yet he always trudged onward.

It was a horrible nightmare with no waking. He became confused, wondering where he was going, uncertain where he was. He could hear himself talking but was unable to understand what he was saying. Other voices were talking, too. A dog barked. Lights seemed to go on in his brain. Blinding lights. Voices. He smiled, dreaming he could hear his uncle Erick speaking to him. He could actually see him, but instead of Erick's usually cocky demeanor, his uncle looked scared, concerned. For some reason the face made him laugh. Tears ran down his cheeks.

Why's everyone looking so sad?

Someone tried pulling Anna out of his arms. Chris grasped her tighter, babbling incoherently. From far off he heard himself cursing, uttering meaningless threats.

"It's okay, son. You can let her go."

Real voices. Red and white flashing lights were everywhere. Something was lifted out of his arms, but he couldn't remember what he'd been carrying. His arms felt light. Light enough to float away. His lips tingled. Again, he felt like he was going to faint.

I can't.

Voices again. Lights were spinning around and around. Erick was speaking to him.

"Erick?" he mouthed the words, but nothing came out. His head swam.

"Just take 'er easy, kiddo."

"On my word," another voice drifted from somewhere far away, "these kids look like they've been to hell and back."

Chris looked into Erick's eyes and finally allowed himself to collapse. Strong arms lifted him; he felt he was floating . . .

~~~ *12* ~~~

THE LIVING AND THE DEAD

WHEN CHRIS WOKE, rays of sunlight were filtering through the thin slats in the window blinds. Watery sunlight seeped into the room, puddling on the bed sheets. He was in a strange place: a small room with bleached-white walls and a high ceiling; a too narrow bed with too many pillows; a tiny table with plastic, institutional-style eating utensils still wrapped in their sealed packages; a chair in which Erick was sitting; and an IV bag hanging from the bedpost, its plastic tube connecting at a white patch taped to Chris's arm. Seeing the IV in his arm helped him recover from his drowsiness a little quicker.

Erick noticed his nephew stirring and stood up by his bedside. He looked tired. Chris managed a weak smile.

His uncle smiled back at him sunnily and said: "Well, look who's finally awake. How you feeling?"

"Okay," Chris whispered hoarsely. "Where am I?"

"Sage Memorial Hospital, buck-o. Where'd you think, the Holiday Inn?"

"Am I all right?" he asked. His thoughts immediately strayed to Anna, but he pushed them away. It just hurt *too much.*

"Yeah. You're gonna be fine. The doctor called it 'acute enervation'; in other words, you're exhausted. Of course, after finding you in the canyon, I could've told you that. I've gotta admit, you had me a little scared."

A nurse flitted into the room, smiled, and stuck a thermometer into Chris's mouth. "Under your tongue," she commanded, lifting his wrist to check his pulse. He dutifully obeyed.

A few minutes later the thermometer was deftly reclaimed, glanced at, shaken. "You're as good as new," she declared with a wink. "If you promise to eat and drink something, we can remove the IV. Are you hungry?"

Chris nodded even though he wasn't. He really didn't like the idea of being hooked up to a plastic tube. He concentrated on looking the other way as the nurse pulled it out. The bandage was peeled back, and the tube was removed painlessly. She smiled again as she scurried out of the room.

"Do you want to rest some more, or do you feel like talking?" Erick asked.

"Talking."

"All right. Well, let's start from the beginning. First off, lucky for all of us, the meetings in Flagstaff ended earlier than I'd expected. I decided to drive back that evening instead of staying the night, even though the hotel was already covered. As I said, lucky for us I came back when I did."

Chris nodded in agreement.

"As soon as I got home," Erick continued, "ol' Murray came running over and told me about the ruins that they had found robbed. Then he went on to tell me about his growing suspicions of our good friend Bob Reeves. The more Murray talked, the more sensible it sounded: Reeves always *coincidentally* happened to be checked in at the Thunderbird during every robbery that's happened in the canyon during the past four years!

"In the meantime, I realized you weren't anywhere to be found, and I asked Murray about it. He said he hadn't seen you since that morning. It was already dark, and I started worrying, trying to convince myself you were just off somewhere with Kee or at Anna's place. I told myself you were all right and went over to Murray's radio to put out an APB on Reeves.

"Since there was still no sign of my funky nephew I called Kee to see if you were over there. Nope. So I decided to drive over to Davidson Charley's hogan, hoping you were spending the night out there again. I got there about 10:00 P.M. Davidson and Arletta were more than a little surprised to see me at their door looking for you. They thought we were on that camping trip. To top it all off, they thought Anna was with *me!* Anna had ridden off early that morning, heading over to our place, and they hadn't seen her since. By then I was getting really worried. Davidson saddled up one of his horses and went out looking for you.

"I got back to the lodge a little after 10:30 and started putting together a search party. The police were here by 11:00. In the meantime, I'd discovered my horse was missing. So I'd pretty well concluded you two were in trouble out in the canyon somewhere. Oh, by the way, we finally found both horses, and they're fine.

"We weren't out there long before it started to rain. And when I say *rain*, I mean *rain*. Within minutes, both Whiskey Creek and Tsaile Creek were flooding. Our vehicles got bogged down in mud, and we had to go back for some horses. But with all the lightning and thunder the horses were too spooked to be any good. Luckily, Murray got ahold of a couple of four-wheelers; they're darn near amphibious. To make a long story short, we found you several hours later. Or I should say, Bill found us. The dog started barking his head off when we were still a half mile off. Good thing the rain had stopped or we probably wouldn't have heard a thing."

Erick looked at him with an odd expression for a moment before continuing. "Bill looked like he was half beaten to death; his fur was matted with blood. And you were carrying on something awful. I thought you'd lost your mind. When I saw Anna in your arms, my heart just about broke. What went on in there anyway? A couple of times you've mumbled in your sleep about voices and faces. It sounded crazy."

Right then, Chris decided that whatever he'd seen and heard during his private nightmare in the ruins and in the tunnel would be kept to himself, for now anyway. After all, he wasn't sure just what really *did* happen.

And Anna. Poor Anna.

He whispered her name. Erick smiled tenderly and nodded.

His heart felt like it was exploding. His lips quivered, and tears filled his eyes. He clutched the arrowhead pendant that he still wore around his neck, his gift from Anna.

"You all right?" Erick asked, putting his hand on his nephew's shoulder. "You want to rest some more?"

Chris shook his head.

"Okay. But you let me know if this gets to be too much for you. There'll be plenty of time to fill you in on everything later. So where was I?

"Oh yeah. You were carrying on like you'd lost your mind. Luckily, you passed out, giving yourself a break. We wouldn't have known what had happened except you came to several times, babbling about ghosts, Mr. Reeves, and helicopters.

Going on what we suspected of Reeves and adding your mumbo jumbo, we pretty much put two and two together.

"Reeves was nowhere to be found. When we checked his room the next morning, we discovered that he had packed up and split. The rest was all Navajo Police work. They traced his car license number and notified the Highway Patrol to be on the lookout. It wasn't long before they found his car deserted up in Tsaile. Also, going on your ramblings about a 'copter, they did a search on pilots' licenses to see if he had one. He did. Both a plane and a whirlybird license. Next, the police put out a bulletin to all the nearby airports to be on the lookout for Reeves.

"Later, Sky Harbor Airport in Phoenix called back to say that a 'copter piloted by Reeves had landed there earlier that morning. The police got on it right away and found out Reeves had also booked a flight to New York City, leaving in a few hours. Probably on his way to do some dealing with auction houses. They apprehended him at the boarding gate; his buddies were picked up at a hotel. The room was full of stolen pottery and other goods—enough to put them away for quite awhile. They're now sitting in the Phoenix City Jail awaiting charges of breaking federal antiquities laws, kidnapping, and . . . "

"And murder!" Chris sobbed. The pain in his heart was too much to bear. "Oh Erick, I tried to save her."

Erick looked startled, confused. Then a dawning expression descended on his face. "Hey, Chris, Anna's *alive*. Somehow you carried her almost all the way out of there. She's doing fine. Actually, better than you. She was released yesterday after begging the doctors to let her go. She was in the room just down the hall from yours."

Chris looked at his uncle dumbfounded, certain he couldn't be hearing this. It was too good to be true. It was impossible, a mistake. He had felt her pulse. He had seen her die.

Erick continued: "That girl's got more than luck on her side. There's a razor-fine trail of a bullet's path running along the back of her head. If she had been turned even a slight bit differently, she'd be . . . well, it wouldn't have been good. Anyway, the blow knocked her unconscious, but the wound was only superficial—not even deep enough for stitches. The worst of it is they had to shave a small area at the back of her head to get a good look at it. Only a very small spot I've been told. But she's so embarrassed about it that she's going around wearing a ball cap all day. Kee was teasing her about it, saying he'd like to shine up her bald spot so he could use it as a mirror. She gave him a look that could've frozen the devil."

Chris laughed with teary eyes. He could just imagine that look. *Alive!*

He couldn't help it. He cried.

Erick's hand rested comfortingly on his nephew's shoulder. "It's all right, son. You did real fine out there. I'm so proud of you—took a man to do what you did."

"Do my parents know I'm here?"

Erick looked down and fumbled with the bed rail. "Nope. And I'll tell you why . . . I held off calling your parents 'cause I knew they'd go nuts with worry. There was no way they could've gotten out here to help with the search, so why put them through all that?

"After we found you, the doctors assured me you'd be all right. I didn't know what to do. Your parents certainly had the right to know what had happened to you, and I knew they oughta know. Maybe I've just been making excuses to myself, but I kept thinking about all the other problems they're dealing with right now and . . . well, I knew they'd fly right out here and want to take you back. Maybe I'm being selfish, but I'm not ready to have you go home yet. I don't think you're ready either; and I know one young lady who'd be very disappointed if her knight in shining armor were snatched away before the end of summer."

Erick looked up at his nephew.

"Thanks," Chris whispered. "I owe ya."

Erick shrugged. "Yeah? Don't mention it. Not now anyway. Just rest up so we can get you out of here soon. I have a day off coming up, and I thought it would be a good time to do our camp-out. I'm tired of hanging around this place—you might as well just get a room here for the summer if you're here much longer."

"What day is it?" he asked.

"Friday."

Chris shook his head, astounded. He had gone into the canyon Wednesday evening. He had slept two days.

"Well, get your rest," Erick said by way of ending his visit. "I'll be around again later." To Chris's surprise, his uncle leaned over and kissed him on the forehead.

"Looks like they're bringing out the food trays. Enjoy," Erick said, poking his finger down his throat. "See you later, buck-o."

After supper, a steady parade of friends showed up. There were a lot of flowers, a lot of cards. Chris couldn't help but think it was a little like being around for his own funeral, although it was nice to feel so cared for.

Kee showed up with Davidson and Arletta Charley. The two older Navajo didn't say much, just smiled and patted his arm a lot. Kee thanked him for his part in disclosing the pothunters, and even more important, for saving his niece. Chris wondered where Anna was, but he didn't ask. Later on, some tourists from the lodge came by to wish him well—some he hardly even knew. He grew tired again and eventually slept. In his sleep, he dreamed.

He again felt the darkness, the madness, the gibbering irrationality. He could see the faces . . . leering and twisting into deformed masses of stretched rock. Bubbling. Writhing. And the voices of the dead began whispering . . .

Suddenly, the dream dispersed with the entrance of a gust of high-energy wind. Anna Joe entered, bringing with her the scent of fresh, outside smells. Her cheeks were flushed; her dark eyes were dancing. On her head was the infamous ball cap. Thick whirls of hair hung loosely over her shoulders, moving like wafts of black smoke. She looked very much alive. Entering behind her was Mr. Murray. Marie followed at his heels, carrying a basket of fruit.

"How's my boy?" Mr. Murray greeted, squeezing Chris's arm and smiling foolishly. "When you breaking out of this place?"

"*Ya et éh,*" Marie hailed, holding up the fruit basket and beaming proudly. "I raided Murray's cooler room, picked out all the best pieces," she boasted.

"Just like her, ain't it?" Mr. Murray said. "Brings you a gift from my supply room and thinks she's being benevolent."

Marie just winked.

Chris laughed.

Between the two adults' bantering Chris was asked a thousand questions: How was he feeling? When would he be released? Had he called his parents yet?

Anna stood back by the chair, quiet, smiling charmingly. During all the teasing and laughter, their eyes frequently locked.

After awhile, Mr. Murray knuckled him on the shoulder and said: "The woman's gonna talk your ear off if I don't get us rolling out of here soon."

Marie elbowed Mr. Murray none too lightly and did her best to look indignant. "Look who's talking!" she said. "A person can't get a word in edgewise with all your prattle."

"Me! Who's always the one lollygagging around at the restaurant? It ain't me," Mr. Murray charged.

New contention began about who lollygagged and who didn't, while they said their good-byes. Anna didn't move until Marie and Mr. Murray were out in the hall; then she walked over to Chris's bedside.

"They're funny aren't they?" she said, fidgeting with a button on her jean jacket.

He nodded.

She looked up, peering into his eyes. "How much did you tell your uncle about what happened in that place?"

"Not much. I didn't know what to tell him. I don't even know what to tell myself. All I know is that it was real. I think we both would agree on that. *Why* it happened, that's something I think I discovered while we were in there."

Anna raised her brow inquisitively.

Chris continued: "You once said that the *chindi* hang around the dead and that the Navajo believe that the dead shouldn't be disturbed. Well, the dead in there were certainly disturbed, weren't they? Think about it. First, a hundred and some years ago Navajo went in there to escape from the soldiers who wanted to round them up and take them away. That would've been a major disturbance, don't you think? Next, you and I come wandering in, inviting more trouble. And then to make things even worse, the grave robbers themselves show up. It was just too much. That's when the whole place started coming apart.

"You should've seen the looks on Reeves's and his goons' faces when they saw the *chindi*. They looked like two little kids lost in a spook house."

They both laughed, relieved it was all over.

"You know, I've been thinking, too," Anna mused. "Maybe I need to listen more closely to my grandfather when he shares his stories. Lately, it's been easy to just kind of tune him out when he gets going

on all that traditional stuff. It's like I've heard it all, over and over. But now, I've been thinking that his stories are more than just old superstitions; they're stories which show me how to live as a Navajo, how to live in harmony with all things, how to respect the ancient places, stuff like that."

"Yeah. Maybe a lot of those old taboos have a purpose; even a *bilagáana* like me could learn something from them."

Anna swatted him lightly on the shoulder. "I doubt it. You're too thickheaded."

Again they both laughed.

"How could you ever explain all this crazy stuff about the *chindi* to anyone?" Chris asked, becoming serious once more.

Anna shook her head. "I don't know. I don't know if I even want to."

Chris didn't say anything. The memories of Coyote Canyon made him shudder.

Anna touched his hand in the silence. "They told me what you did." Tears welled up in her eyes. Chris could feel his own eyes getting moist.

"I think you're brave," she whispered. "You saved my life. I can hardly believe you carried me all the way out of there! You're the best friend I ever had." Suddenly, she kissed him—just a light peck on the cheek—and then she disappeared.

Her face had been close to his for only a second or two, but that night he dreamed of how her eyes had looked during that unforgettable moment.

Thunderbird Lodge, Sunday

It was one of those perfect Arizona days, a day when a cloud wouldn't dare show itself in the crystal clear sky. A light breeze, just strong enough to bend the delicate blades of grass in front of the lodge, greeted Chris as he walked over to the parking lot.

Anna sat on her motorcycle, waiting impatiently. Already helmeted, she watched him approach, her eyes smiling. Bill, of course, was sitting nearby. The dog was still wearing a bandage wrapped around his head, looking like he was auditioning for a part in *Red Badge of Courage.*

Chris put on the helmet she offered him and asked: "Where we going?"

"Sheepherding."

"On this?"

She shrugged. "Why not? Anyway, we've got to get going. I'm late."

"Anna . . . late?" he teased. "That couldn't be!"

Anna gave him one of her notorious scowls before jumping up to kick-start the old motorcycle. Chris laughed, the sound of it disappearing beneath the whine of the engine. He laughed some more, enjoying the sheer, simple pleasure of it.